It was my fault he was in danger. I might be dead, but I still had to live with myself, and if I walked away, Josh would suffer. Maybe die.

"I'm at the bottom of a ravine, aren't I?" I blurted desperately, my eyes pleading for him to listen. "In a black convertible. In your dream."

Josh's mouth dropped open. "How do you know that?"

I licked my lips, feeling the heat come up off the road like the fires of hell. I knew better than to break the false memory Ron had given Josh. But he wasn't here, and I didn't know how to reach him. "Because it wasn't a dream," I said.

Once Dead, Twice Shy

A NOVEL

KIM HARRISON

SCHOLASTIC INC.
New York Toronto London Auckland
Sydney Mexico City New Delhi Hong Kong

ISBN 978-0-545-44682-2

12 11 10 9 8 7 6 5 4 3 2 1   12 13 14 15 16 17/0

Printed in the U.S.A.   23

First Scholastic printing, January 2012

Typography by David Caplan

For Andrew and Stuart

ACKNOWLEDGMENTS

I'd like to thank my editor, Tara Weikum, who helped me more than she might know, and my agent, Richard Curtis, who continues to surprise me by what he sees before I do.

Prologue

Everyone does it. Dies, I mean. I found this out for myself on my seventeenth birthday when I was killed in a freak car accident on my prom night. But it was no accident. It was a carefully planned scything, just a small moment in the battle between light reapers and dark, heaven and hell, choice and fate. Only I didn't check out of my life like most dead people do. Thanks to a mistake, I'm stuck, dead on earth. The angel who failed to protect me and the amulet I stole from my killer are the only things keeping me from ending up where the dark reapers wanted me to be. Dead, that is.

My name is Madison Avery, and I'm here to tell you that there's more out there than you can see, hear, or touch. Because I'm seeing it, hearing it, touching it, living it.

One

I leaned my shoulder against a rough boulder and fumed. Dappled sunlight shifted upon my sneakers as the wind made my hair tickle my neck. The sound of kids swimming at the nearby lake was loud, but the happy shouts only tightened the knot in my gut. Leave it to Barnabas to try to turn around four months of failed practice in a mere twenty minutes.

"No pressure," I muttered, glancing across the dirt path to the reaper standing against a pine tree with his eyes shut. Barnabas was probably older than fire, but he blended in nicely, with his jeans, black T-shirt, and lanky physique. I couldn't see his wings, which we'd flown in on, but they were there. He was an angel of death with frizzy hair and brown eyes, who wore a pair of holey sneakers. *Would that make them holy holey sneakers?* I wondered as I nervously rolled a pinecone back and forth under my foot.

Feeling my attention on him, Barnabas opened his eyes. "Are you even trying, Madison?" he asked.

"Duh. Yes," I complained, though I knew this was a lost cause. My gaze dropped to my shoes. Yellow with purple laces, and skulls and crossbones on the toes, they matched the purple-dyed tips of my short blond hair, not that anyone else had ever made the connection. "It's too hot to concentrate," I protested.

His eyebrows rose as he looked at my shorts and tank top. I actually wasn't hot, but nerves had made me jittery. I hadn't known that I was going to summer camp when I'd slipped out of the house this morning and rode my bike to the high school to meet Barnabas. But for all my complaining, it felt good to get out of Three Rivers. The college town my dad lived in was okay, but being the new girl sucked eggs.

Barnabas frowned at me. "Temperature has nothing to do with it," he said, and I rolled the bumpy pinecone under my foot even faster. "Feel for your aura. I'm right in front of you. Do it, or I'm taking you home."

Kicking the pinecone away, I sighed. If we went home, whoever we were here to save was going to die. "I'm trying." I leaned against the boulder behind me, reaching up to hold the black stone cradled in silver wire that hung around my neck. At Barnabas's impatient throat-clearing, I closed my eyes and tried to imagine a hazy mist surrounding me. We were attempting to communicate silently with our thoughts. If I could give my thoughts the same color as the haze around Barnabas, my thoughts would slip through his aura and he would hear them. Not an easy thing to do when I couldn't even see his aura. Four months of this odd student/teacher relationship, and I couldn't even get to stage one.

Barnabas was a light reaper. Dark reapers killed people when the probable future showed they were going to go contrary to the grand schemes of fate. Light reapers tried to stop them to ensure humanity's right of choice. Having been assigned to prevent my death, Barnabas must have considered me one of his more spectacular failures.

I hadn't gone gentle into that good night, however. I had whined and protested my early death, and when I stole an amulet from my killer, I'd somehow saved myself. The amulet gave me the illusion of a body. I still didn't know where my real body was. Which sort of bothered me. And I didn't know why I'd been targeted, either.

The amulet had felt like fire and ice when I'd claimed it, shifting from a dull flat gray to a space-deep black that seemed to take in light. But since then . . . nothing. The more I tried to use it, the more stonelike it was.

Barnabas had now been assigned to shadow me in case the reaper who'd killed me came back for his amulet, and I'd gone back to living as normal a life as I could. Apparently just the fact that I had been able to claim it without blowing my soul to dust made it—and me—rather unique. But watching over me wasn't Barnabas's style, and I knew he couldn't wait to get back to his soul-saving work. If I could just figure this thought-touching thing out, he could resume his regular duties, leaving me reasonably safe at home and able to contact him if the dark reaper showed up again. But it wasn't happening.

"Barnabas," I said, weary of it, "are you sure I can do this? I'm not a reaper. Maybe I can't touch thoughts with you because I'm dead. Ever think of that?"

Silent, Barnabas dropped his gaze to the pine-rimmed lake. The worried lift to his shoulders told me he had. "Try again," he said softly.

I tightened my grip until the silver wires pressed into my fingers, trying to imagine Barnabas in my thoughts, his easy grace that most high schoolers lacked, his attractive face, his riveting smile. Honest, I wasn't crushing on him, but every angel of death I'd seen had been attractive. Especially the one who'd killed me.

Despite the long nights on my roof practicing with Barnabas, I hadn't been able to do anything with the shimmery black stone. Barnabas had been hanging around so much that my dad thought he was my boyfriend, and my boss at the flower shop thought I should take out a restraining order.

I pushed myself away from the rock. "I'm sorry, Barnabas. You go on and do your thing. I'll sit here and wait. I'll be fine." Maybe this was why he'd brought me. I'd be safer waiting for him here than several hundred miles away—alone. I wasn't sure, but I think Barnabas had lied to his boss about my progress in order to get out and working again. An angel lying—yup, it happened, apparently.

Barnabas pressed his lips together. "No. This was a bad idea," he said, crossing the path to take my arm. "Let's go."

I jerked out of his grip. "So what if I can't push my thoughts into yours? If you don't want to leave me here, then I'll follow you and stay out of the way. Jeez, Barnabas. It's a summer camp. How much trouble can I get into?"

"Plenty," he said, his smooth, young-looking face twisting into a grimace.

Someone was coming up the path, and I rocked back a step. "I'll stay out of the way. No one will even know I'm there," I said, and Barnabas's eyes crinkled in worry.

The people were getting closer, and I fidgeted. "Come on, Barnabas. Why did you fly us out here if you were just going to take me home again? You knew I couldn't solidify in twenty minutes what I've been trying to do the past four months. You want this as much as I do. I'm already dead. What more can happen to me?"

He looked up the path at the noisy group. "If you knew, you wouldn't be arguing with me. Hide your amulet. One of them might be the dark reaper."

"I'm not afraid," I said as I tucked it behind my shirt, but I was. It wasn't fair, being dead and still having to deal with heart-pounding, breath-stealing tension when I was afraid. Barnabas said the sensations would fade the longer I was dead, but I was still waiting, and it was embarrassing.

Eyes down, I dropped back to let three girls and three guys go by. They were in flip-flops and shorts, the girls chattering as if they didn't have a care in the world as they headed downhill to the dock. It all seemed normal—until a shadow passed over me and I looked up.

Black wing, I thought, stifling a shudder. They looked like crows to the living—when the living noticed them at all. The slimy black sheets were nearly invisible when viewed from the side but for an oddly bright, shimmering line. These scavengers fed on souls of the people taken by the dark reapers, and if it wasn't for the protection of my stolen amulet, they'd be all over me. Light reapers stayed with a scythed soul, protecting the deceased until they could be escorted from the earth.

I glanced at Barnabas, not needing to hear his thoughts to know that someone in the group was targeted for an early death. To find out who it was would be a mix of the sketchy description from Barnabas's boss, and Barnabas's intuition and ability to see auras.

"Can you tell who the victim is?" I asked. From what Barnabas had told me, auras had a telltale shimmer as to a person's age—which sort of gave Barnabas an excuse for why he had failed in protecting me. It had been my birthday, and he only worked with seventeen-year-olds. I'd been sixteen until right before the car flipped, and officially seventeen when I actually died.

Barnabas squinted, his eyes silvering for a moment as he drew on the divine. It totally creeped me out. "I can't tell," he said. "Everyone is seventeen but the girl in the red swimsuit and the short, dark-haired guy."

"How about the reaper, then?" I asked. No one was wearing an amulet—but since the stones could shift to look like anything, it didn't mean much. Just one more skill I didn't have.

He shrugged, still watching them. "The reaper might not even be here yet. His or her aura will look seventeen, just like ours. I don't know all the dark reapers by sight, and I won't know for sure until he or she pulls their sword."

Pull sword, stick it in a person, reap accomplished. Nice. By the time you knew who the threat was, it was too late.

I watched the black wings sport above the dock like gulls. Beside me, Barnabas fidgeted. "You want to follow them," I said.

"Yes."

It was too late to give the prevention to someone else. The memory of my heart seemed to pound harder—a shadowy remnant of being alive my mind couldn't let go of yet—and I grabbed Barnabas's arm. "Let's do this."

"We're leaving," he protested, but his feet were moving, and I watched his sneakers meet the earth in perfect synchronization with mine as we headed downhill.

"I'll just sit quiet. What's the big deal?" I asked.

Our steps echoed hollowly on the dock, and he drew me to a

stop. "Madison, I don't want to make another mistake," he said, turning me to face him. "We're leaving. Now."

I looked past him, squinting in the brighter light and the fresh wind, shuddering when one of the slimy sheets of dripping black alighted on a pole—waiting. Oblivious, the group argued with the dockmaster. If we left, someone was going to die. I wasn't leaving. I took a breath to convince Barnabas I could do this, but from the dockmaster's hut a voice called, "Hey! You guys doing anything?"

Barnabas jumped, and I turned, smiling. "What's that?" I called back, tension hitting me.

"Skiing," the short, dark-haired guy said, holding a pair. "We can't take two boats unless we have eight people. You two want to be the designated watchers?"

A quiver rose through me. "Sure!" I said, sealing the deal. Barnabas wanted this. I wanted this. We were going to do this.

"Madison," he griped.

But everyone was enthusiastically piling into the boats, and I dragged him closer, scanning the faces to see who didn't fit. "Which boat has the victim on it? I'll take the other."

Barnabas's jaw was clenched. "It's not that easy. This is an art, not a memo."

"Then guess!" I pleaded. "For criminy's sakes, even if we're on different boats, you'll be like what . . . thirty feet away? What is the big deal? I'll just shout for you, okay?"

He hesitated, and I squinted at him, watching his thoughts play over his face. Bad idea or not, a life was on the line. Behind me, the black wing took flight.

Barnabas took a breath to say something, pausing when a guy in gray trunks came over. He held a towrope and was smiling. "I'm Bill," he said, extending his hand.

I turned sideways to Barnabas and took it. "Madison," I said shyly. I figured he wasn't the reaper. He was too normal-looking.

Barnabas muttered his name, and Bill looked him up and down. "Do either of you know how to drive?" Bill asked.

"I do," I said before Barnabas could think of an excuse to get us out of here. "But I've never pulled a skier. I'll just watch." I glanced at Barnabas. That last bit had been for him.

"Great!" Bill smiled devilishly. "You want to ride in my boat? Watch me?"

He was flirting, and I grinned. I'd been holed up with Barnabas for so long, working on this thought-touching stuff, that I'd forgotten how fun—and how normal—flirting was. And he was flirting with *me*, not the girl on the dock who'd stripped to a yellow bikini to show off her butt or the stunning girl with the long black hair, who was wearing shorts and a brilliantly patterned top.

"Yeah, I'll watch you," I said, taking a step after him, only to jerk to a halt when Barnabas snagged my arm.

"Hey," he said loudly, his eyes silvering again and making

me shiver. "Let's do guys on one boat, girls on the other."

"Cool!" bikini girl said cheerfully, not seeming to notice his metallic-like irises, though she was looking right at him. "We get the blue boat."

I pulled out of Barnabas's hold, uneasy that I could see something that the living clearly couldn't. I didn't think even Barnabas knew I could see it. The level of noise increased as they rearranged themselves, boats starting to chug and lines being cast off. Still on the dock, I pulled Barnabas down so I could whisper, "Bill isn't the reaper, is he?"

"No," he whispered back. "But something's hazing him. He might be the victim."

I nodded and Barnabas turned away to talk to a guy in a blue shirt standing possessively behind the wheel of the red boat. Saying hi to the girls, I landed at the bottom of the small blue speedboat. Barnabas's plan must be to shadow the victim. I looked across the dock at Bill, wondering if I could see a dark haze about him, or if it was my imagination.

All too soon, we were on the water, speeding over a small lake with the girl in the red one-piece skiing behind our boat, and Bill behind the other. The rhythmic thump and the hissing of the shattered waves was like a familiar, glorious song. Sunshine beat heavy on my shoulders, its warmth stolen by the force of the wind whipping my hair into my eyes. The black wings had risen up in confusion at the dock, but the biggest were already making their way after us. My unease grew as I dropped my gaze to the skiers.

Bill looked like he knew what he was doing, as did the girl behind our boat. If they weren't dark reapers, and the guy in the gray trunks driving wasn't a reaper, then that left three possibilities, two of whom were with me. I resisted the urge to finger the black stone hiding behind my shirt, hoping that Barnabas hadn't put me on the wrong boat. Bikini girl had on a necklace.

"Are you a good skier?" I shouted to her, wanting to hear her talk.

She turned and smiled, holding her long blond hair tightly. "Not bad," she said, leaning in to be heard over the engine. "Think she'll fall soon? I'm dying to get on the water."

My smile went stilted, and I hoped she wasn't foretelling her future. "She might. The jump is coming up."

"Maybe then." She glanced at the purple tips of my hair, dropping her gaze to my skull-and-crossbones earrings. Smiling, she said, "I'm Susan. Cabin Chippewa."

"Uh, Madison," I said, holding tight to the boat with one hand as my balance shifted. It was too windy to really talk, and as Susan watched the skier behind us jump our wake, I assessed the driver.

The petite girl behind the wheel had an enviable mane of black hair, long and thick. It streamed out behind her to show little ears, strong cheekbones, and a placid expression as she looked forward. Wide shoulders and a slim body made her seem as capable as she was attractive. Her Hawaiian top was glaring out here in the sun, making me wish I had worn sunglasses, too.

My attention shifted across the water to the red boat thirty yards off our starboard and Barnabas talking to the guy in the blue shirt. The wind shifted as the boat turned to the jump, and Susan leaned in, her long hair smacking my face before she grabbed it. The black wings had caught up. All of them. "How long are you here for?" she asked.

"Uh, not long," I answered truthfully. "School starts up in about two weeks."

Susan nodded. "Same here."

I shifted on the spray-splattered vinyl, nervous. I was supposed to be the designated watcher, but I really wanted to watch the driver. No mortal had a right to be that gorgeous. If I could find the guts to talk to her, I might be able to tell if she wasn't. *And what if she isn't, Madison?* I thought, growing nervous. It wasn't like I could tell Barnabas. Maybe splitting up hadn't been such a good idea.

"My parents made me come here," Susan said, pulling my attention back. "I had to leave my job and everything," she added with an eye roll. "Lost a month of pay. I work at a newspaper, and my dad didn't want me staring at a computer screen all summer. They still think I'm twelve."

I nodded, my expression freezing when a kite-sized sheet of dripping black glided between the boats as if we were standing still. Stifling a shudder, I sent my gaze to Barnabas; I could see his frown from here. Frolicking both above the water and under it, the black wings grew close, winding my tension tighter, starting at my feet and climbing higher.

Susan stood and wobbled to the bow of the boat to glory in the wind. In a surge of worry, I forced my hand down from the black, water-washed smoothness of my amulet and held my middle. I was getting seasick, not from the jarring boat, but from what was going to happen. Unless Barnabas could do a better job than he had with me, someone would die. I'd done that—well, half of it, anyway—and waking up in the morgue wasn't fun.

My gaze slid from the skier to Barnabas as the red speedboat inched closer; we were nearing the jump. His brown hair streamed back from the wind, and he was talking to the driver, his knees spread wide for balance, looking every bit like the casual seventeen-year-old he was trying to save. As if feeling my attention, Barnabas looked up and our eyes met. Between us, a black wing dove into the water. *Son of a dead puppy.* They were getting bold. It was almost time.

"Hey!" Susan shouted, looking to where the black wing had vanished. "Did you see that?" she asked, eyes wide. "It looked like a stingray. I didn't know they had stingrays in freshwater."

Because they don't in this hemisphere, I thought, scanning the horizon. Black wings were everywhere, keeping pace with the boats above and below the water.

Susan gripped the gunwale with two hands as she stared at the water off the starboard. She clearly wasn't seeing half of what was out there, but she'd noticed something. My illusionary pulse quickened. The more anxious I became, the more my mind relied on memories of being alive. Something was about to happen, and I didn't know what to do. What if that beautiful girl at the wheel was the reaper?

Tense, I listened to the water hiss as we raced past the ski jump. Our skier took it, letting out a war whoop at the top of her arc. She lost her balance on the landing but fell into the water gracefully, as if she knew what she was doing.

Bill, moments behind her, shied off at the last second. The toe of his ski snagged the ramp. I gasped, helpless as he pinwheeled. Reapers loved to work by accident, adding a deathblow to an already injured person to hide their actions. Barnabas had been right. The victim, and hence the reaper, must be on his boat. "Turn around!" I shouted. "Bill hit the jump."

Our boat shifted, and Susan grabbed the rail. "Oh my God!" she cried. "Is he okay?"

He'd be fine as long as Barnabas got to him first. I glanced at our driver as she turned the boat, silently urging her to hurry up. Her eyes were now showing over her sunglasses. *Blue,* I first noted, and then fear slid through me. Even as I watched, they shifted to silver as she smiled in quiet satisfaction. She was a reaper. *The driver was the dark reaper.* Barnabas was on the *wrong* boat. Damn it, I knew she was too pretty to be alive.

Scared, I forced my eyes down before she could see that I knew. Edging to the back of the boat, I clasped my arms about myself, becoming frantic as we slowed. Our skier was swimming toward Bill, but Barnabas had dived into the water and would get there first. Susan joined me at the side of the boat when Barnabas slipped his arm around Bill to start pulling him to my boat, not his. The fear in me deepened. He didn't know the reaper was with me. He was bringing him right to her! Damn it, why had I insisted on doing this when I couldn't even communicate with Barnabas!

The two boats were coming together, the engines softening to a chugging rumble that died when they were both turned off. Everyone was at the edges, shouting. I tried to get Barnabas's attention without alerting the dark reaper that I knew who she was—all the while not letting her out of my sight. But Barnabas never looked up.

Hands went down to Bill. He was conscious but bleeding from a head wound. Coughing, he weakly extended a shaky hand for help. I shivered when the shadow of a black wing slid over me and was gone. Beside me, Susan shuddered as well, clearly feeling but not seeing the dripping black sheets above us. "Get him up," I whispered, thinking they looked like sharks gliding smoothly under the surface. "Get him out of the water."

My boat, though, wasn't any safer, and I lurched to get between the dark reaper and Bill as he was lugged over the edge and a wash of water soaked the plastic green rug. The dark reaper had to know someone was here to stop her, though she probably thought it was Barnabas, since he was the one who'd jumped in.

"Is he all right?" Susan said, letting out a little yelp when our boats gently hit and the driver of the red boat threw a rope to tie us together. Dropping to her knees in the narrow space before the back bench seat, Susan yanked a beach towel from her bag. "You're bleeding. Here, put this on your head," she said, and Bill blinked vacantly at her.

Crouched beside Bill, Barnabas wasn't looking at me, and my heart hammered as I inched closer to a beautiful death in a Hawaiian top and flip-flops, smelling faintly of feathers and an overly sweet, cloying perfume. *She won't recognize me. I'm safe,* I tried to convince myself. But when Barnabas stood and started to make the jump to the other boat to leave me, I lost it.

"Barnabas!" I cried, then froze as I felt, more than heard, the hiss of metal through air.

Tension slammed through me, and I whipped my head around. The dark reaper stood with her feet planted firmly apart in the narrow space up front, the light shining gloriously upon her and her sword. It had a violet stone above the grip that matched the one around her neck. I could see it now. Both stones blazed with a deep intensity. She wasn't looking at Bill. She was looking at Susan.

"No!" I shouted, panicked. There was a flash of light against a blade, and, unthinking, I lunged to get between them, hitting Susan with my shoulder to send her sprawling. Yelping, she fell beside Bill at the back of the boat. My knees burned as they hit the plastic carpet. Looking up, I was blinded by the sun reflecting upon a moving blade, and I gasped as it sliced cleanly through me with the sensation of dry feathers against my soul.

It was as if time stopped, though the wind still blew and the boat still bobbed. The people on the other boat broke from their shock and started shouting. Oblivious to them, the dark reaper stared at me, her lips parted in horror when she realized she'd scythed the wrong person. "By the seraphs . . ." she whispered as the confused babble rose higher.

"Damn it, Madison," Barnabas said, his voice clear over the rest. "You said you were just going to watch."

Still kneeling before her, I splayed my hand against my unmarked middle and remembered the awful feeling of when I'd sat dazed in a flipped car at the bottom of a ravine, shaken but alive. And then the helpless terror when the dark reaper had pulled his sword, meeting my confusion with his anger because I hadn't died in the crash and he had to kill me with his own blade.

"Uh, you missed," I said as I shook off the memory of my death.

Susan staggered up, and the dark reaper dissolved her blade, sending its power back into the stone around her neck. Her lips parted when her gaze found my amulet resting against my chest, shaken from its hiding place by my fall. "Kairos's stone!" she said. "You have Kairos's amulet? How? He's . . ." She hesitated, peering at me in confusion. "Who are you?"

Who the devil is Kairos? I thought. Seth was the dark reaper who'd killed me. Licking my lips, I got up, almost stepping on Bill. "Madison," I said boldly, scared to death. "I took an amulet, yeah. Leave, or I'll take yours, too."

It was an idle threat, but the reaper's expression went from surprise to determination. "If you've got Kairos's amulet, he probably wants it back," she said, her slim hand reaching for it.

"Madison, get away from her!" Barnabas shouted.

Frightened, I backpedaled, tripping over Bill and landing on the long bench seat at the back. Face grim, she followed. Sure, she couldn't kill me again, but she could drag me off.

People shouted, and a blur darted between us. It was Barnabas, and I stared, gaping as he suddenly stood before me and the dark reaper in his perfectly average jeans and T-shirt, dark and dripping from the water. His presence was overwhelming—the stance of a warrior. "You'll not have her," he intoned, looking at the dark reaper from under his wet curls.

"She has Kairos's amulet," the dark reaper said, and with a violet pulse from her amulet, a blade was again in her hand. "She belongs to us."

What did she mean, *belongs to us*? I shrank back into the stiff cushions, but Barnabas had created his own blade, pulled from the power of his amulet, now glowing a violent orange. The two clanged as they hit, followed by a deep thrum echoing between my ears. From around us came the noise of frightened people scrambling back, trying to get out of the way.

Swiftly, Barnabas stepped forward and swung his weapon against hers in a rasping spin, violet and orange streaks of light marking their paths. The dark reaper's blade was torn from her hand, arcing through the air to slide cleanly into the water with hardly a ripple.

Shocked, she hunched over, holding her wrist as if she had been stung. Her amulet was as dark as her expression. Someone swore a muffled oath of a question.

"Get back," Barnabas said. "I've heard of you, Nakita, and you're out of your depth. Don't reap in my sphere. You'll fail every time."

The dark reaper's eyes narrowed. Jaw clenched, she looked at Susan, then me. "Something's not right. You know it. I hear it in the seraphs' songs," she said, and when Barnabas's chin rose, she dove into the water to retrieve her blade.

Seconds passed. The dark reaper didn't surface, but if she was like Barnabas, she didn't need to breathe and was likely gone.

The guy in the blue shirt darted to the back of his boat and looked down. "Did you see that?" he said, spinning from the water, to us, and the water again, his eyes wide. "Did you freaking *see that*?"

Barnabas took a breath to speak, losing his mien of wrathful warrior on his exhale when he changed his mind. The light reaper's eyes met mine, and I cringed when the silver sheen was replaced by worry.

From the corner of the boat, Susan asked, "Did you just shove her in the water?"

Whoops. This might be kind of hard to explain.

Barnabas grimaced, and with his hand gripping his amulet, he calmly said, "Who?"

Bill was staring at the sky, his gaze clearly tracking the dispersing black wings.

Susan's expression became confused. "There was a girl," she said, sitting up. "She had black hair." Susan looked at Bill. "And a knife. It was a knife, wasn't it? You saw it, right?"

Taking the towel from his head, Bill looked at the red stain and said, "I saw it."

Barnabas walked with perfect balance through the boat and dropped to one knee before Bill. "I didn't see anything." Still holding his amulet, he peered into Bill's eyes as he put the towel back against his cut. "You hit your head pretty hard. You feel okay? How many fingers am I holding up?"

Bill didn't answer, and I looked over the water, avoiding Barnabas's gaze. His eyes had gone silver again, and I thought to look now would be a mistake. "Bill hit his head," Barnabas said calmly. "He needs to go to the dock and get it looked at."

Like magic, the fear and confusion turned to concern as everyone rearranged themselves on the two boats. My knees were shaking as Barnabas got our boat started, and in the sudden noise, I leaned into him. "They won't remember?" I asked, not realizing he had the skill to change memories.

Barnabas slid out from behind the wheel. "You drive," he said shortly. Putting a hand on my shoulder, he pushed me into the seat. "Hurry up before someone remembers you didn't drive out here."

He sounded peeved and I started fiddling with the levers. Yeah, I could drive a freaking boat. I'd grown up in the Florida Keys and had been able to put a boat in a slip before I could ride a bike.

Barnabas was stowing the skis and wet ropes when I shifted into a slow crawl. The other boat had taken off fast, and I followed its path to make the ride easier. Susan was on her cell phone, shouting, "He hit his head on the ski jump! Camp Hidden Lake. The one with the big red canoe over the road? We're headed for the dock. He's awake but needs stitches, maybe."

Edging into a faster speed, I pressed into the cooling vinyl and felt my shoulder go cold where Barnabas had touched it. The black wings were gone, apart from a single smudge skirting the edge of the lake. The scythe had been prevented, but Barnabas wasn't happy.

Closing her phone, Susan wobbled back to sit beside Bill at the back of the boat. "Hey," she said, shouting over the engine noise. "I've got an ambulance coming. You doing okay?"

He was flushed and he looked confused. "Where's the girl

with the sword?" he asked, and I caught Barnabas making the "crazy" sign, twirling his finger beside his ear.

"Take it easy," Susan said, softer, but still almost yelling. "We'll be there in a minute."

The lights of the ambulance at the dock gave me a point to aim at, and I slowed our speed as we closed in. People had gathered, and I hoped Barnabas and I could make our escape before we were noticed.

"Where's the girl with the sword?" Bill asked again, and Barnabas went to sit on his other side.

"There is no girl with a sword," he said tightly.

"I saw her," he insisted. "She had black hair. You had a sword too. Where's your sword?"

I glanced back and Barnabas gave me a tired look, making me feel like I'd really messed this up. Maybe having to change people's memories was a sign of sloppiness.

"Just relax, Bill," the light reaper was saying. "You hit your head hard."

I gripped the wheel tighter and wondered if Bill's head injury made him less susceptible to having his memory changed. Just how badly had I screwed this up? Jeez, all I'd done was shove Susan out of the way. I wasn't going to just stand there and let her be killed. Susan was blissfully ignorant. She was alive. She would finish her life and probably do something great with it, or she never would've been unfairly targeted by the dark reapers in the first place.

My furrowed brow eased, and I pulled a strand of spray-damp hair out of my eyes. I was glad I'd intervened, and nothing Barnabas could say would convince me it hadn't been the right thing to do. I couldn't help but feel a little sheepish, though. Two years of martial arts practice, and all I'd done was shove her out of the way?

Barnabas left Bill and Susan clustered together on the back bench and sat in the seat across from mine. "I put in for a guardian angel," he said as he leaned close enough for me to catch the scent of sunflowers at dusk. "Susan will be fine."

"Good." I eased the throttle down as we neared the dock, refusing to drop his gaze. "That wasn't so bad, was it?"

Leaning back, he huffed. "You have no idea the trouble you caused," he said. "Saints protect you, Madison. Five people saw her cut right through you. Five people I have to cobble alternate memories for. You think thought-touching is hard, you should try altering memories. I shouldn't have brought you. I knew it wasn't safe."

I clenched my teeth and stared at the approaching dock, thick with people. "I saved her life. Wasn't that the point?"

"You were identified by a reaper," he said darkly. "You said you'd simply observe, and you go and . . . get recognized! They know the resonance your amulet gives off now. They can follow it. Find you."

I took a breath to protest. Reapers had amulet resonances; living people had auras. Either could be used by reapers to find people both at a great distance and close-up, sort of like a noisy fingerprint or photo. "Are you telling me I should have let her die, Barney?" I said bitterly, knowing he hated the nickname. "Let that reaper cut her down just so I wouldn't get recognized? Call Ron. He can change my amulet's resonance. He has before."

Arms crossed over his chest, Barnabas frowned. I was right, though, and he knew it. "I'm going to have to, aren't I?" he said, sounding like the seventeen-year-old he was masquerading as. "I haven't been pinged in three hundred years. Apart from your reap, that is. I need to get my resonance changed, now, too." Sullen, he stared ahead. A sullen angel. How sweet.

But the more I thought about it, the worse I felt. It seemed that ever since I'd made his acquaintance, I'd been screwing up his life. My special talent. Now he had to call on his boss to fix things, and I knew he hated looking bad. "Sorry," I said softly, but I knew he heard me.

"Until we get the resonance of our amulets changed, we're as vulnerable as ducks sitting on the water," he muttered.

Chilled, I looked for black wings, but they were gone. The water reflected the trees close to the dock, flat in the lee of the wind, and I shifted the engine into neutral. "I said I'm sorry," I said, and Barnabas looked up from the flashing ambulance lights.

His brown eyes were black in the shade, and it was as if I was seeing them for the first time, finding something different in their depths. "There's a lot you don't know," he said as I swung the boat around to dock beside the first. "Maybe you should start acting like it."

Susan was flipping the bumpers out over the side, and Barnabas moved into the bow to throw the front dock line when I cut the engine to drift in. The ambulance crew was waiting with a stretcher, and they seemed relieved when Bill shouted that he was okay. There was an air of efficient excitement, and when I saw the bright polo shirt that said camp counselor more than a laminated tag would have, I cringed. We had to get out of there.

The boat emptied out amid loud chatter and requests for information that Susan was delighted to supply at the top of her voice. I stood, wanting to go home, but Barnabas couldn't simply pop us out in front of everyone. He stepped onto the dock, and I followed, nervous in the crush.

"Keep an eye on the girl," he said as I fidgeted. "I need to find some quiet so the guardian angel can locate me. It's not likely they'll try for her again, but it's possible. Especially if they know you're here. Don't do anything if a reaper shows, okay? Just yell for me. Can you do that?"

Subdued, I nodded, and he wove through the people on the dock. I slowly followed to find a place out of the way near the ambulance. My heart had stopped again. Finally. Barnabas thought it was funny, which only made it more embarrassing. I was always taking in air I didn't need, too. Susan was within earshot with a cluster of girls and a camp counselor. It was an odd feeling, wanting to be close but afraid to be included.

Susan's story was bringing gasps from the surrounding people, but I was glad to hear nothing about sword fights or girls in Hawaiian tops disappearing under the waves. At night, when she was asleep, it might be a different story. I'd seen too many haunted looks on my dad's face that made me wonder if he remembered the morgue. While I was busy stealing an amulet from my killer, my dad had gotten the phone call telling him I was dead. Finding him alone in my room, sifting through my things before he knew I was alive, had been heartbreaking. And his joy when he saw me breathing? I'd never been hugged so hard. Though his memories had been shifted . . . sometimes, I thought he remembered.

Barnabas had settled himself atop a red picnic table under the pine trees. A vaporous softball-sized light hovered before him, looking everything like the imperfections you see in pictures from time to time. Some people thought the glows were ghosts, but what if they were guardian angels, only seen when the light was right and they were caught on film?

"And then he fell back in the water," Susan said, words slowing when something didn't jive with her memory, and I turned away lest she see me and ask me to back her up. She had mentioned that she worked at a newspaper—maybe a planned journalism career was why she'd been targeted. Perhaps she was supposed to do something later in life, something that would work contrary to the dark reapers' great plan. That's what the whole game was about. That's why I'd been killed. I didn't know what great thing I was supposed to have done, and now that I was dead, it was likely I never would.

Arms crossed, I leaned against the prickly solidness of a tall pine tree, and vowed I wouldn't *ever* feel bad about saving Susan's life.

Barnabas stood, and I watched him weave his way through the crowd with that ball of light trailing behind him. Susan's friends noticed him, and, giggling, they hushed themselves. Pretending ignorance, Barnabas smiled and shook Susan's hand. As if it was a signal, the hazy light shifted from him to her. She had her guardian angel; she would be safe. A knot of worry eased in me.

"Thanks for keeping him talking out there," Barnabas said, brushing his wet hair aside in a casual show that made someone in the back sigh. "You should go to the hospital with him. He's going to have to stay awake all night in case he has a concussion."

Susan flushed. "Sure. Yes. You think they'd let me?" She turned to the counselor. "Can I go?"

At the chorus of catcalls and a yes, Susan flashed a smile and jogged to the ambulance. The haze of light entered the ambulance before Susan, and Barnabas's faint tension vanished, telling me that he, too, had been worried about her. It just seemed like he hadn't cared.

Feeling better, I looked at him and smiled, glad it was over. The reaper's face went blank and my smile faded. He turned on a heel and walked off, expecting me to follow.

Head down, I wove through the diminishing crowd after him, my satisfaction at having saved Susan stilling to a gray ash. If I had had another way home, I'd have taken it. Barnabas looked ticked.

Two

The air in the upper reaches had been frigidly cold, and my wet hair felt frozen when Barnabas landed us right where we'd started this morning: New Covington High's rear parking lot. As usual, his wings had vanished in a swirl of back wind before I got a good look at them, replaced with dry jeans, a casual black T-shirt, and a gray duster totally inappropriate for the hot weather but totally suitable for making him look good. The soft color reminded me of his wings as it draped over his shoulders and fell to his heels.

Unsure, I wove through a few cars to get to the bike rack. The vehicles hadn't been here this morning, and I wondered what was up. It took me two tries to get the combination right, and I slowly wheeled my green ten-speed back to the shade and Barnabas, propping it against the waist-high wall between the steep hillside and the main road before I slumped against it to wait for Ron, Barnabas's boss.

I missed my car, still back in Florida with my mom, but the lack of a vehicle had been more than made up for by the chance to get to know my dad again. Mom had sent me up here because she'd had it with teacher/principal/parent chats and worrying when the phone rang after dark that it would be a cop. Okay, so maybe I had been a little enthusiastic in "exerting my freethinking tendencies," as the school counselor had told my mom, right before he privately told me to quit acting out for attention and grow up, but it had all been innocent stuff.

A cicada whined from somewhere, and I scrambled up onto the wall beside Barnabas and crossed my arms over my chest. Immediately I put them down, not wanting to look pensive. Barnabas looked pensive enough for both of us. His grip on me on the flight back had been uncomfortable. He'd been quiet too. Not that he ever talked much, but there was a stiffness now, almost a brooding. Maybe he was annoyed that he got wet jumping into the lake. My entire backside was damp now, thanks to him.

Uneasy, I pretended to fix my shoelaces so I could shift an inch or so away from him. I could've asked him to drop me off at home, but my bike was here. Not to mention I hadn't wanted nosy Mrs. Walsh to catch sight of Barnabas sprouting wings and flying away. I swear, the woman had binoculars on her windowsill. School had been the only place that I'd thought no one would see us. Why there were cars here now was beyond me.

I dug my phone out of a pocket, turned it on, checked for missed calls, and tucked it away. Glancing at Barnabas, I said, "I'm sorry I got you identified on your reap."

"It wasn't a reap. It was a scythe prevention."

His voice was tight, and I thought that for someone who'd been around for so long, he could sure act childishly. Maybe that was why he was assigned to seventeen-year-olds.

"I'm still sorry," I said as I picked at the top of the cement wall.

Leaning against the wall, Barnabas put his squinting gaze on the sky and sighed. "Don't worry about it."

I drummed my nails on the hard cement as again the silence descended. "It figures the beautiful one would be the dark reaper."

Barnabas brought his gaze back to me, affronted. "Beautiful? Nakita is a dark reaper."

My shoulders went up and down in a shrug. "You guys are all gorgeous. I could pick one of you out in a crowd just by that." His face showed surprise—as if he'd never noticed how perfect they all were. When he looked away, I added, "You know her?"

"I've heard her sing before, yes," he said softly. "So when she used her amulet to make her scythe, I could put a name to a face. She's been a dark reaper for a long time to have a stone so deep a shade of violet. They slowly shift color with experience, light reapers going down through the spectrum from green, to yellow, to orange, and finally a red so deep it's almost black. Dark reapers go the other way, up through the blues and purples to violet. The color of your stone is reflected in your aura when you use your amulet. But you can't see auras yet, can you?"

That had been positively catty, and if I hadn't been thinking about my own stone, black as space, I would have told him to shut up.

"So she's been at this longer than you," I said, and he turned to me in wonder.

"How do you figure that?" he asked, sounding insulted.

I glanced at his amulet, a flat black now that he wasn't using it. "It's like a rainbow. She's violet, and you're orange, a step away from red, way on the other side of the rainbow. You're not red yet. You get red, and you'll be as experienced as her."

He looked me up and down, his stance going stiff. "My amulet is not orange. It's red!"

"No it isn't."

"It is so! It has been since the pyramids."

I waved a hand dismissively. "Whatever . . . I still don't get how hearing her sing comes into it."

With a huff, he turned to the parking lot and away from me. "Amulets make it possible to communicate beyond earth's sphere, and I've heard her. The color of the stone and the sound of her singing match. Sort of like hearing an aura instead of seeing it. From there, it's not hard to guess who's singing because there are so few of us within the earth's sphere to begin with. And although I can hear dark reapers, I can't make out what they are saying. Nakita would have to shift the color of her thoughts to match my aura for that, and we are so far apart in the spectrum that it would be almost impossible. Besides, why would I want *her* thoughts in mine?"

My eyebrows rose. That bit of information might have been helpful as I spent the last *four freaking months* trying to learn how to use my amulet. "Huh. I thought you just . . . popped up to heaven or something when you wanted to talk."

His head drooped. "It's been aeons since I took up an amulet and became earthbound."

He's earthbound? "Whoa," I said, gravel grinding under my shoes as I shifted to face him. "Reapers are earthbound?"

"No, only light reapers are earthbound," he said, flushing in what looked like embarrassment. "Nakita is free to come and go. She touches the earth only long enough to kill; then she leaves."

That had sounded rather bitter. "I thought all angels lived in heaven."

"No," he said shortly. "Not all of us."

Making a face, he ran a hand over his frizzy hair, turning it even more untidy, in a charmingly attractive way. "Few angels transgress, but those who have often take a reaper path to make amends. And when they absolve themselves, they return to their other duties."

Amends? Absolution? Barnabas was a reaper because he'd gotten in trouble? And here I was, getting him in more of it. I suppose saving lives would look good on any angel's résumé. "What did you do?" I asked.

Barnabas crossed his arms and leaned against the wall. "I'm a light reaper out of a sense of moral responsibility, not because I displeased the seraphs. I don't care what they think."

I'd heard Barnabas swear by—or at—seraphs before as we sat on my roof and pitched stones at the bats. I knew all too well he didn't think much of the high muckety-mucks in the angel realm, but I couldn't help but wonder what the seraphs did. I suppose it took a lot to run a universe.

Still not looking at me, Barnabas pushed off the wall and moved to stand at the edge of the light. He wasn't telling me something, a feeling that grew when he put his hands on his hips and stared out at the hot parking lot. "She's right, though. Something smells worse than a black wing in the sun," he said, almost to himself. "Nakita said you have Kairos's stone. That's not possible. He's . . ." Barnabas turned, chilling me with his expression. "Madison, I've been thinking. When Ron comes, I'm going to ask him to give your instruction to someone else."

My lips parted, and I felt like I'd been socked in the gut. Suddenly it made a lot more sense. *He's giving up on me. God, I must be more stupid than I thought.* Hurt and not knowing what else to do, I slid off the wall, scraping the back of my legs when I didn't push out far enough. Tears pricked at my eyes, and, grabbing my bike, I started for the distant entryway. I was going home. Ron could find me there.

"Where are you going?" Barnabas said as I swung my leg over my bike.

"Home." Being dead sucked. I couldn't tell anyone, and now I was going to be passed around like a Christmas fruitcake no one wanted. If Barnabas didn't want me around, that was fine with me. But to stand there while he told Ron was humiliating.

"Madison, it's not that you're failing me. I can't teach you," Barnabas said, his brown eyes holding both worry and sympathy.

"Because I'm dead and stupid. I got that part," I said miserably.

"You're not stupid. I can't teach you because of whose amulet you've got."

His words held a scary amount of concern, and I stopped, suddenly frightened. In all this time, Ron had never been able to figure out what kind of amulet I'd taken. "Kairos's amulet?" I whispered, then stiffened at the sudden tickling between my shoulder blades. I froze, my gaze darting to the shadows, wondering if they hadn't just jumped forward. Barnabas's gaze went behind me, and his expression turned to an odd mix of relief and caution.

"I've only got a moment. Let's see your amulets," came the timekeeper's distinctively crisp voice.

I spun to see a small man squinting in the sun. "Ron," I said softly as he strode forward, his loose gray robes just as bad as Barnabas's duster in terms of being totally wrong for the heat. I glanced at the school, hoping no one saw me with them. I had a bad enough reputation already for being weird. Six months, and I was still the new girl. Maybe I should start dressing down. No one else had purple hair.

Chronos—Ron for short—looked like a cross between a wizard and Gandhi, having a martial arts–like robe and brown eyes that gave me the impression he could see around corners. His eyebrows were blond from the sun but his skin and tightly curling hair were dark. Shorter than me, he nevertheless had a huge presence about him. It might have been his voice, which was deeper than one would expect. He had a pleasant, crisp accent, as if he had a lot to say and not a lot of time to say it.

He moved fast, too, and had an amulet that allowed him to tap into the time stream and kept him from aging, since unlike the reapers, timekeepers were human for some reason. Which begged the question of how old he really was. He used his ability to manipulate and read time to help the light reapers. It was through him that Barnabas got his scythe-prevention assignments.

Glancing sourly at the sky, Ron held out his hand, fingers wiggling. "Madison?"

"Ron, about my amulet," I started, holding it before the timekeeper, still on its leather lanyard around my neck.

"Yes, I know. I'm going to fix that," he muttered as his fingers blurred out of existence for a moment, encircling my amulet. I felt a tingling across my scalp, and then it was done. "When did you dye your hair?" he said lightly, his sharp gaze not meeting mine.

"After prom. Ron—"

But he was already standing before the light reaper, his hand held out in a possessive fashion. Barnabas looked positively ill as he towered over the small man. "Barnabas . . ." the man intoned with warning, or recrimination maybe. I think Barnabas heard it too, since he took his amulet from around his neck and handed it over instead of coming closer. Without his amulet, Barnabas couldn't make a scythe, losing much of his abilities. Without mine, I'd be a ghost, more or less.

"Sir," Barnabas said, looking uncomfortable as his amulet took on the same hue it had when his sword was bared; then it returned to a matte black. "About Madison's amulet . . ."

"It's fixed," Ron said smartly as he handed Barnabas's back.

Barnabas looped the simple cord back over his neck and tucked his amulet behind his T-shirt. "The dark reaper at the scything recognized it."

"I know! That's why I'm here! You were identified," Ron barked, fists on his hips as he peered up at him, and I dropped my eyes, chagrined. "Both of you. On her first scythe prevention. What happened?"

Great, I'd gotten Barnabas in trouble again. "I'm sorry," I said contritely, and Barnabas's head came up. "It was all my idea," I gushed, thinking that if I took the blame, Barnabas might give me another chance. My knowing that auras had sounds might make all the difference in our practice, and maybe then we'd be able to accomplish thought-touching. "Barnabas didn't want to take me until we could thought-touch, but I convinced him it wasn't that big of a deal. And then I met Susan. I couldn't let that reaper kill her. It happened so fast."

"Stop!" Ron barked, and I jumped. The man's eyes were wide, and he was staring at Barnabas—who was . . . cringing? "You told me she could thought-touch!" the small man accused, and my mouth dropped open. "You lied? One of my own reapers lied to me?"

"Uh," Barnabas stammered, backing up when Ron stepped forward to get in his face. "I didn't lie!" he yelped. "You assumed she could when I said she was ready. And she is."

He thinks I'm ready? Even when we can't thought-touch?

Ron's eyes narrowed. "You knew I wouldn't allow her on a prevention until she could touch thoughts. Because of it, five memories had to be shifted. *Five!*"

My brief elation that Barnabas had thought I was ready evaporated, and I wished I'd kept my mouth shut. Puppy presents on the rug, this sucked.

"It doesn't matter how much we practice, Madison will not be able to touch thoughts with me," Barnabas protested, his face going red. "It's her amulet, not her!"

"Good God almighty," Ron interrupted, turning away with a hand in the air. "I can't keep this from the seraphs. Can you imagine the fervor? You simply haven't spent enough time with her. Learning how to thought-touch is done slowly, not *bang* and you can do it."

Barnabas's eyebrows furrowed. "I never said she wouldn't be able to learn how to touch thoughts with someone, just not me. Sir," he said, glancing at me, "Nakita was the dark reaper assigned to the scything. She recognized Madison's stone. Madison has Kairos's amulet!"

The timekeeper went stock-still. Alarm turned to wide-eyed surprise. Seeing his gaze touch upon my amulet, I put my fist around the stone so firmly that the silver wires cradling it bit deep. It was mine. I'd claimed it and no one was going to get it without a fight. Not even Kairos, whoever he was.

"Kairos?" Ron whispered, and then, seeing my fear, he broke eye contact with me.

"Yes, and if she has Kairos's amulet," Barnabas said, "then maybe—"

"Hush," Ron whispered, cutting his words off, and Barnabas fumed. "I knew it wasn't a regular reaper's stone, but Kairos's? Are you sure that's what Nakita said?"

Barnabas was standing stiffly. "I was there, *sir*."

Nakita also said I belonged to them, which makes me feel all peachy-keen. I just wanted to be who I was before, blissfully ignorant about reapers and timekeepers and black wings. Maybe if I ignored it, it would go away.

Ron squinted at us, his stiff stance giving off a sudden air of mistrust. He gestured to the edge of the shadow. "Go watch the sky, Barnabas."

Silent, Barnabas shifted to the edge of the sun and sent his gaze upward. A chill went through me. Everything had changed in an instant—because of Kairos.

"Who's Kairos?" I asked, turning my attention back to Ron.

"My counterpart." Ron had his hands on his hips as he looked uneasily out from the shelter of the tree and into the hot parking lot. "Light reapers, dark reapers. Light timekeeper, dark timekeeper. You didn't think I was the only one, did you? Everything has a balance, and Kairos is mine. Kairos watches the threads of time weave into possible futures and sends dark reapers to scythe people early. I spend more time trying to second-guess him than anything else."

He said the last word like it was a curse. My heart was pounding again, and I crossed my arms over my chest as if I could make it stop. Okay. I had swiped a timekeeper's amulet. Crap, I had to get rid of this thing, but it wasn't like I could borrow a reaper's amulet and return this one to Kairos. Keeping it was my only option. I'd never sleep again. Good thing I didn't need to.

"No wonder Seth hasn't come back," I said, trying to work this through to a conclusion. "I bet he's hiding from Kairos."

Frowning, Ron shifted deeper into the shadow to lean against the wall beside me. "A reaper wouldn't be able to use Kairos's amulet, just as a timekeeper can't use a reaper's," he said. "Nakita must be mistaken. Unless"—Ron's eyebrows rose in a private thought as he turned sideways to look at me—"it wasn't a reaper who killed you. Perhaps Kairos was doing a little extracurricular scything on his own."

Barnabas looked over his shoulder at that, and Ron waved him to be quiet. Again.

"What did *Seth* look like?" Ron asked, his voice deceptively mild.

Nervous, I levered myself up to sit on the wall, glancing at Barnabas, but he had returned his gaze to the sky. I drew my knees to my chin, not wanting to remember that night, but the memory came back with crystal clarity. "Dark complexion," I said. "Dark wavy hair. Nice accent." *Good kisser,* I added in my thoughts, cringing. *Oh, God. I've kissed the guy who killed me.*

Sexy stranger at the prom had turned into psychopath Seth, a dark reaper bent on killing me. Which he did, using a reaper blade after rolling his convertible down an embankment hadn't done it. I'd woken up in the morgue that night to hear Barnabas arguing with another light reaper as to whose fault it was I was dead. They'd been there to apologize and keep the black wings off my soul until I got to my "reward." But everything changed when Seth showed up at the morgue as well. Seems he wanted to throw my soul in front of someone to "buy his way to a higher court," whatever that meant. But only Barnabas and I knew that last part. For some reason Barnabas had thought we shouldn't say anything about it to Ron. And then I'd stolen Seth's amulet, and the fact that I'd been able to do that at all and remain here was a mystery to everyone involved.

Ron rubbed his ear like he had a nervous tic. "Taller than you by about a hand?"

My stomach clenched. "Yeah," I mumbled, "that's him."

Barnabas's feet shifted in the grit as a long exhale escaped Ron. "I should be blessed by baboons!" Ron muttered, then started pacing within the confines of the shade. "That was Kairos," he said tightly. "He didn't give you his true name. God, if you ever loved me, open my eyes for me when I'm being this stupid!"

"But he looked *my* age," I protested. Great, not only had I kissed the man who killed me, but he was older than the pyramids, too. *Yuck!* Now that I thought about it, he had been too good at both dancing and kissing to be seventeen.

"Kairos gained his position unusually early, long before his predecessor intended." Halting, Ron stared into the parking lot. "Hasn't aged a day since acquiring the amulet now around your neck. Pretty prima donna. I bet he's not happy about growing older again. I'd wager a timekeeper's amulet is the only divine stone you could have claimed that wouldn't blow your soul to dust."

"Because I'm dead?" I guessed, and Ron shook his head.

"Because you're human. Just as timekeepers are."

"So it really isn't my fault then that I couldn't keep her alive," Barnabas interrupted. "I can't best a timekeeper."

"No, you can't," Ron said, giving him a look that said to shut up. "And if Madison has bonded with Kairos's stone, the only way he can reclaim it is if she's dead."

"But I *am* dead," I protested, hands clasped about my drawn-up knees.

Ron smiled faintly. "I mean, your soul destroyed. He's got your body, I presume. Someone has it. And as long as you exist in some fashion, the amulet is tied to you. That you were able to claim it at all from him is a miracle." He glared at Barnabas when the reaper tried to interrupt. "You need to stay away from him," he said, turning back to me.

"Not a problem," I said, scanning the sky I could see. "Just tell me what cloud he lives on, and I'll make a note of it."

Ron resumed pacing, his robes moving elegantly and his slight form staying in the tree's shade. "He lives on earth, same as me," he said distantly, clearly too preoccupied with his thoughts to get the joke.

"Sir," Barnabas said, making me nervous when he turned his back on the sky. *Shouldn't someone be watching?* "If Kairos hasn't come after her by now, maybe he won't."

"Kairos give up on his quest for immortality? No. I doubt that," he said. "I'm guessing he hasn't come after Madison yet because until today, no one knew he'd lost his amulet. He was undoubtedly taking the time to make another one. The longer he spends on it, the better it will be—though he'll never create one that matches the power of the one he lost. No, Nakita has probably told him Madison has it. He'll be looking for her now. We will have to hope I changed your resonance fast enough."

"Timekeepers make the amulets?" I asked, surprised, and my attention fell on Ron's own black amulet, almost lost in the folds of his robe. "Can't you make me a new one and I can give Kairos his amulet back?"

Ron blinked at me as if startled by the thought. "I make them, yes, and give them to angels who are stirred to take action and choose to become something they've never been before. Not everyone is happy with the way things are, and this is one way of many to make a difference. But you're dead, Madison. I can't create a stone to keep the dead alive. Trying to use one I've given to a reaper will burn through your human mind. I say since Kairos killed you, you have the right to keep his. Of course, the seraphs may think differently."

I bit my lower lip worriedly when Barnabas moved his attention to the road at the top of the hill as a car went by. Seraphs. They had the clout to make big decisions. Reapers were below them, and guardian angels lower. Barnabas talked about seraphs like they were spoiled children with power. Scary. "This is bad, isn't it?" I offered softly.

Ron's bark of laughter died quickly. "It's not good," he

said; then, seeing my pinched brow, he smiled. "Madison, you claimed Kairos's stone. It's yours. I'll do my best to see that it stays that way. Just give me the time to get the political machine working."

I slid from the wall, nerves demanding I move. "Ron, I know why he's after me now, but this started months ago. What did I *ever* do to make him come after me in the first place?"

Barnabas turned from the edge of the shadow to face us, but Ron interrupted him before he could speak, coming forward to take my hands and smile reassuringly. At least I think it was supposed to be reassuring. But there was something in the back of his eyes that made me queasy.

"I have a few ideas," he said, his gaze touching mine briefly before darting away. "Let me find out more. No need to worry you needlessly."

"Ron, if she has Kairos's stone, then perhaps—"

"Oh, look at the time," Ron blurted, taking Barnabas's arm and actually jerking the reaper off balance. "We have to go."

Go? Go where? Startled, I took a step forward. "You're leaving?"

"We'll be back soon." Ron squinted as he dragged Barnabas into the sunny patch. "I have to talk to the seraphs, and I'll need Barnabas as a go-between." He smiled, but it looked strained. "I'm not dead yet, you know," he said with forced good humor. "I don't have a direct line to the divine plane. No need to worry, Madison. Everything is fine."

But it didn't feel fine. Things were happening too fast, and I didn't like it.

"Sir!" Barnabas exclaimed as he yanked out of Ron's grip. "If Kairos comes after her, changing her amulet's resonance won't be enough. He knows what she looks like. So does Nakita. Either of them can simply walk around and find her. Shouldn't we leave her with a guardian angel?"

Ron blinked as if shocked that he hadn't thought of that himself. "Uh, of course," he said as he came back into the shade. "What a perfectly proper thing to do. But, Madison," he said as he gripped his stone and a glow of black light leaked from between his fingers, "I'd advise saying nothing about Kairos's amulet to your guardian." His eyes went to my amulet and then back to my gaze. "The fewer who know you have it, the fewer I will have to convince you should be allowed to keep it."

Frightened, I nodded, and he smiled. Almost before my head stopped moving, a faint sphere of golden light hazed into existence in the shade of the oak tree. I stared at the dancing, hovering glow. It had to be a guardian angel. *For me?* Barnabas was clearly relieved, and I wondered why he cared when he'd been so hot to get rid of me not twenty minutes ago.

The ball of light shrank to nothing when it landed atop the wall, and I started when an ethereal voice seemed to insert itself into my head, saying, "Guardian, Reaper-Augmented Cherub, Extinction Security, as requested!"

Patting my shoulder, Ron turned, apparently having heard it as well. "And you are?"

"G.R.A.C.E.S. one-seventy-six," the curious chiming came again, making my ears hum.

Cherubs? As in flying naked babies with arrows?

Barnabas looked worried and the ball of light reappeared as the voice belligerently shot out, "You got a problem with cherubs, reaper?"

"No," Barnabas said. "I didn't think G.R.A.C.E.S. employed the cherub union until the protected was eighteen."

A tiny rude snort filled my mind. "Like anyone is going to fall in love with *her*?" the light scoffed. "I'm a guardian angel. Not a miracle worker."

"Hey!" I exclaimed, insulted, and the globe of light darted to me. I backed up when it got too close. Graces, eh? More like a firefly from hell.

"You can see and hear me?" the ball of light chimed as it ran a quick circle around me, and I spun to try to keep it in view.

"Hear, yes. See? Not really, no." Disoriented, I stopped turning, and the glow settled on the bars of my bike and faded away. Barnabas snorted, and the glow reappeared and dimmed.

"Delightful," Ron drawled. "One-seventy-six, this is a temporary duty, not till death do you part. Keep her safe, and I want to know immediately if anything unsavory should come within thirty cubits of her."

The light lifted from the bike and shifted to me. "Thirty cubits. A-a-a-affirmative!" .

Affirmative? This is an angel, right?

Ron gave me a last warning look to behave, grabbed Barnabas's arm, and started pulling him away. "I'll be back when I can. Oh, and I like your hair. It's very . . . you."

I tried to smooth out my brow as I fingered the tips of my hair, then jerked when the two of them vanished. My breath hissed in, and I actually saw the shadows shift to later in the day. Not by much. Maybe a few seconds was all, but Ron had stopped time to cover his tracks. My stone was warm as if in reaction to his own amulet, and I held it tight. Looking out from the shade into the bright parking lot, I thought the world looked a whole lot more dangerous.

For the first time in four months, I was alone.

Three

"*I hate it when he does that,*" I muttered, jumping when my guardian flew in front of me.

"Does what?" it chimed out.

Maybe not so alone. Sighing, I reached for my bike. "Stops time and jumps the sun like that, but I really wasn't talking to you." If anyone saw me talking to the air, I'd definitely end up in the weirdo clique when school started back up. Not my senior year. I didn't have time to work myself out from *that* again. You come to school one day with bat wings for Halloween, and you never live it down. A faint smile curved my lips up. Wendy, my friend back in Florida, had worn them too. It had almost made the batgirl-twins jokes funny.

The ball of light made a burst of indignant sound. "You're really short, for a mortal."

"Look who's talking," I shot back, then swung my leg over my bike. I shoved on the pedal, and the wheels made a pained sound, resistance keeping me from moving. "Hey!" I exclaimed when I realized my front tire was flat. The guardian angel was laughing. It had to be; its color was wildly shifting through the spectrum. "What did you do to my bike?" I said, though it was obvious.

"I'm protecting you!" it sang merrily. "Don't you feel safer already?"

My thoughts went to the five-mile walk home. "Protecting me from what?" I snapped. "Me being thought of as anything other than a dweeb?" Ticked, I pushed my bike across the hot pavement toward the distant exit. Stupid guardian angel. What the devil was wrong with it?

I spun around at the sound of the metal school door crashing open, and saw a guy wearing running shorts come out. Two more people followed him. Track practice in August? "There once was a girl with blond hair, whose tresses were short like a mare," G.R.A.C.E.S. one-seventy-six sang, hovering by my ear. "She brushed and she preened, like she was a queen, till I laced her shampoo with some Nair."

"Charming. It sings," I muttered, and the angel giggled, seeming to send a wash of cool air over me. Behind me, voices rang out amid the thumping of car doors and starting engines. The first truck roared by me, and I turned to the right to avoid the exhaust, pulling my bike past the end of the wall and dragging it up the hill to the main road.

Someone blew their horn, and I ignored it. The hill was steep, and when a line of erosion bushes appeared in front of me, I angled into the water runoff ditch full of rocks the size of my head. But the moment I found the ditch, my front tire got stuck and the handlebar jammed into my gut. My breath came out in a pained huff, and I looked up to find a truck stopped at the top of the hill. Great. I had a freaking audience.

"There once was a girl with a bike, who thought she'd go off on a hike."

"Shut up!" I shouted, then looked up to the sound of a door slamming. My shoulders slumped and I felt weary. It was Josh. Prom-date Josh. The same guy who'd only gone out with me because my dad and his dad worked together and had set it up. I'd been a "favor." And when Josh accidentally let this slip at the prom, I'd left in a huff—with Seth/Kairos. Swell. I hadn't seen much of Josh since I'd died except for passing him in the hall. Now, leaning against my bike, I watched him recline against his truck door with his ankles crossed, smiling at me.

Oh, for cripe's sake. Looking back down, I laboriously unstuck the wheel and pushed forward, but the memory of the night I died filled my thoughts. Josh had followed me to make sure I got home okay even after I'd ditched him. He'd seen the car crash, had slid down the embankment to try to save me. I think he'd even held my hand as I died. Barnabas assured me he didn't remember a thing. Except perhaps that I'd been a bitch

51

to him at prom and left with someone else.

"You need some help?"

I looked up to find Josh still leaning against his truck. He looked good, his wet blond hair dark from a shower, blue eyes squinting in the sun as he pushed a new pair of trendy glasses back up his narrow nose. I'd seen him talking with the drama club geeks at school and sticking up for the smart kids in the hall, but he usually hung with the jocks. Not quite the popular crowd, but close enough not to matter in a town this size. He was nice to everyone, which was not the norm for what I'd call a very dateable guy.

"I said, do you need some help!" he said louder as he waved at a girl driving by. It was Amy. I didn't like her. She was too full of herself to have room for a real thought in her head.

Blowing the hair out of my eyes, I wished I was still at the lake, dark reaper and all. "No," I called back. "But thanks." Head down, I shoved the bike over a rock and moved up a foot.

"Are you sure?"

Why is he being nice to me?

From above and a little behind me came a high voice saying, "Listen, I just thought up the end of it. There once was a girl with a bike, who thought she'd go off on a hike. She headed off west, 'cause she thought it was best, but ran into someone she liked."

My foot slipped. Habit pulled my breath in fast when my

ankle gave a twinge and the bike fell down the six inches I had managed. "I'm going south, not west," I grumbled, then looked up at Josh as the angel laughed at me. It was too hot to feel guilty for past bitchiness. "I changed my mind," I said loudly. "I could use some help."

Josh pushed himself away from his truck and started down, sliding until he found the rocks and began to pick his way. I waited, then backed up when he gave me a smile and took the handlebars from me.

"How did you get a flat tire?" he asked as he snuck glances at my purple hair.

"There once was a girl from the shire, who constantly got a flat tire."

"Shut up!" I yelled, then cringed when Josh turned to me, shocked.

"Uh, not you," I amended, just about dying on the spot. Not that I could, but I felt like it. "I, um, wasn't talking to you."

Josh's eyebrows went up. "Who were you talking to? Dead people?"

He meant it as a joke, but I felt myself pale. From behind me came a chiming, "You have to be alive first, short stuff, to be dead."

The silence stretched, and Josh's expression went from amused to bothered. "It was a joke, Madison."

Miserable, I tried to find a spin on this that wouldn't make me look like Mad Madison. Stupid guardian angel. This was all its fault. "I'm sorry," I said, tucking my hair back. "It was nice of you to stop and help me. I really appreciate it. I'm just hot." My tension eased when his jaw unclenched. "It hasn't been a good day," I added.

Josh was silent, and I glanced at him. We were almost to the top, and I didn't want him to leave thinking I'd yelled at him for no reason. "You're, uh, on the track team, right?" I said.

"Yup. We're doing a charity relay tomorrow at the school carnival," he said, slowing to work the front tire between two rocks. "Dollars per time around the track, that kind of thing. Coach thinks it's a great way to keep us from going soft over the summer. What are you doing to help?"

"Me?" I stammered. "Uh . . ."

Josh looked askance at me. "That's why you were at the school, right?"

"Not really," I said. "I was meeting someone. They left. My tire went flat." The angel edged into my vision, and I slapped at it. "Wow, big mosquito," I said, and it hummed in indignation, the light shifting brighter.

"And you came here because you didn't want your dad to find out you were meeting someone?" Josh said. "Gotcha." Sighing, he looked to the top of the hill as if he was distancing himself from me already.

I was screwing this up royally. "It's not my dad; it's my neighbor," I said.

"Mrs. Walsh?" Josh asked, startling me.

"You've heard of her?" I said, finding myself grinning at his understanding smile.

He nodded. "My friend Parker lives on your street. That woman goes through his garbage to pull out the recyclables. Creepy old bat."

"That's awful." Feeling better, I dropped my eyes. "I didn't expect to get a flat tire. I mean, it's only five miles to my house . . . you know." Puffing beside Josh with the bike between us, I glanced at him, wishing I hadn't yelled at the guardian angel. Josh was silent as we reached the top, and as soon as we were both on level ground, I reached for the handlebars, nervously trying not to touch his fingers. "Thanks," I said as I looked at his truck parked on the side of the road. He was going north, and I was going south, into town. "I think I can get it from here."

Josh's hands slipped from the chrome. "Is everything okay? You're kind of jittery."

I jerked the bike from him. "I'm fine. Why?"

He shoved his glasses up. "Your hair is wet, and I know you weren't on the track. Did someone give you a swirly or something? You're acting like my sister when she's in trouble and the world is out to get her."

I felt cornered, and my pace quickened. "No more trouble than usual," I said with false cheerfulness. A car whizzed by. It was the last of the track team. Cripes, I missed my car.

Josh was silent, his steps slowing as we got farther from his truck. "Look, I know how dads can be. Mine keeps such a tight leash on me I can't take a leak without him checking to see that I washed my hands."

Halting, I looked up. "It's not my dad. He's cool."

"What is your problem?" Josh said. "I'm just trying to help."

My eyebrows rose when the ball of light made a kissing sound. "He's trying to he-e-e-elp," it crooned, and Josh shivered when it landed on his shoulder. Great, the thing belonged to the cupid union. This was not what I needed.

"I'm fine. Really. Thanks," I said shortly, shoving my bike through the loose gravel.

"Well, I'm not," he said darkly, and I kept going. "Listen, I'm not trying to hit on you, but I've been having these dreams about you for the last three weeks and it's freaking me out."

I stopped, unable to turn around. *He's dreaming about me?*

"There once was a poet from Plunket—"

I swung at the angel as if going for a fly, and with a little ping of sensation, I hit it. It arced across the road with a faint yelp, and I stared at Josh. *He's dreaming about* me?

"Never mind," he said, turning away. "I gotta go."

"Josh."

He waved his hand at me, but he didn't look back as he trudged over to his truck.

"Josh?" I called again, then stiffened at the shadow that raced over the ground between us. My eyes went up as fear sliced through me. A black wing. Here? *What the devil?*

"Josh!" I shouted. *Son of a dead puppy.* Somewhere in my town, a reaper walked. Hunting. Hunting me? But Ron had changed my resonance!

The sour tinkling of bells told me my angel had returned. "How long is a cubit?" I asked the angel breathlessly as Josh neared his truck.

"About a foot and a half," it said tightly. "You got grass stains on my dress. You're a nasty person, you know that?"

Dress? It's a girl, then.

"Why?" she asked, and then she tinkled in understanding. "Oh, nice. Black wings. Don't worry. They can't sense you if I'm nearby. I've got a field of immunity. It's like you're not even there."

"Yeah, I've got it too," I said. "But if they can't sense me, then why are they here?"

"Him, I think. Yes. Him. Someone's hunting him."

My eyes widened. *Him? She means Josh? Why?* And then I got it. My amulet resonance had been changed too late. Nakita had followed me back, at least as far as Three Rivers, but lost me when Ron shifted things. And since neither she nor Kairos would stand on a street corner and wait for me to walk by, they were trying to find me by hunting someone I might be with. Kairos had met Josh at the prom. Talked to him. Saw him and his aura. They were tracking me down through Josh—the only person both Kairos and I knew.

"Call Barnabas," I said to the angel, frightened.

"Can't do that," she said lightly. "I'm not experienced enough to touch thoughts with anyone. I'm a first-sphere guardian angel."

"Then go get Ron," I said to her, seeing the black wing start to circle.

"Can't do that, either." Whirling about my head, she sent flashes of light into my eyes. "I'm instructed to keep you safe and report reapers. You're safe."

"What about Josh?" I asked, and she hummed as if she didn't care.

Josh's truck's door creaked open, and I panicked.

"Josh!" Shoving my bike along, I awkwardly ran down the center of the empty road. "Josh, I'm sorry," I gushed as I reached the driver's door and grabbed the open window. "Wait." My heart pounded as I looked up, but the black wing had started to veer off already. My tension eased, then shifted to worry. The angel wouldn't protect him, but if I stayed with Josh, he'd be under my immunity. If the black wings couldn't sense him, then neither could Kairos or Nakita. Why hadn't I worked harder on thought-touching? It sure would be handy about now.

Josh sat with his hands on his wheel, staring at me as a car drove slowly around us. "Madison, you are one weird dudette."

"Yeah, I know," I rushed. "Give me a ride to the bike shop? I need a new tire."

Cocking his head, Josh looked at me. I'd do just about anything right now not to have to explain, but I'd also do anything to keep him safe. It was my fault he was in danger. I might be dead, but I still had to live with myself, and if I walked away, Josh would suffer. Maybe die.

"I'm at the bottom of a ravine, aren't I?" I blurted desperately, my eyes pleading for him to listen. "In a black convertible. In your dream."

Josh's mouth dropped open. "How do you know that?"

I licked my lips, feeling the heat come up off the road like the fires of hell. I knew better than to break the false memory Ron had given Josh. But he wasn't here, and I didn't know how to reach him. "Because it wasn't a dream," I said.

Four

Seeing as how it was about twenty years old, Josh's truck was spare in the amenities. It had manual locks, manual windows, a long bench seat, and no air conditioner. It had a monster of a stereo, though, and he had to move a crate of CDs to the middle before I could get in. Hard rock, mostly, and some classic rockers my dad listened to. Wendy would have liked the harder stuff. He hadn't turned the music on, and I was getting nervous from the ongoing silence.

A Harley bell hung from the radio knob, and my guardian angel had parked herself on it with a satisfied hum the moment she followed me in. I swear I'd heard her singing when Josh did a three-point turn and headed us into town, the bell swinging softly.

His gym bag was shoved under the seat, and the narrow

space behind the front seat held an expensive-looking fly rod. I couldn't help but wonder why Josh drove an old truck when I knew his dad could afford a lot better.

He was a good driver, silent as we made our way to the bike shop. His curiosity as to how I knew about his dream had gotten me a ride, but now he seemed to be waiting for me to elaborate. I didn't quite know what to say as I sat beside him, and I leaned forward into the sun to look out the front window for black wings. There was only blue sky, which made me feel better. No black wings meant no reapers. The one always followed the other.

"What are you looking at?" Josh asked, and I leaned back.

"Nothing." The old truck bounced as we went over a bridge, and the homes started to shift to businesses. He was waiting for me to say something. Since we only had about five stoplights to go, I sighed. "What do you remember about the prom?" I asked softly.

"That you were a real—" His words cut off, and his neck went red. "Uh."

"I was nasty," I finished for him, wincing. "I'm sorry. I was mad when I found out you'd only asked me to the prom because your dad wanted you to, because my dad was worried about me being new to town and not knowing anyone. I was a class-A bitch."

"No, you weren't," he said, but I could tell he was still mad about it. I remained silent, and he added, "You left with someone

I didn't know, and I went home early. That's it."

My fingers played with the weather stripping around the open window as I hesitated, and he slowed as the traffic thickened. "I left with a guy you'd never seen before," I said softly, "but you followed us to make sure I got home okay."

Josh's grip shifted, as if I'd said something he'd never told anyone else.

"That was sweet of you," I said, and he swallowed, making his Adam's apple shift. "I was being stupid. I was mad at the world for my mom shipping me up here. What happened wasn't your fault." I took a slow breath as I found the next words. "He drove right off the road. The car rolled to land right side up at the bottom of a hill." My grip tightened as Josh stopped at a four-way, and I put a hand to my middle. I didn't feel so good.

"He had a sword," Josh said, then crossed the intersection. "In my dream, I mean."

His voice had gone defensive, like he didn't believe it, and I moved my hand to my knee to hide the scrape the boat's carpet had given me. "The crash didn't kill me," I continued, "so he, uh, yeah. He scythed me. I don't remember anything after that until I woke up in the morgue."

Josh made a noise of disbelief. "Nice, Madison," he scoffed. "So now you're dead."

The glow around the Harley bell brightened, and the guardian angel blurted, "Oh my God in heaven, you *are* dead. Why am I guarding a dead person?"

Ignoring her, I gripped my amulet tight as she buzzed up to look at it. "Oh-h-h-h!" she hissed, her glow almost going out. "Kairos is going to go supernova. Does he know you have his amulet? Where did you get it? Did Chronos give it to you? How did *he* get it?"

I squinted through her glow at Josh. *Crap.* This was not going well. She wasn't supposed to know. Ron was going to be ticked. But as long as she was with me, she couldn't leave to blab it around. Josh was shaking his head. I lifted my chin angrily. "Okay then. Tell me what you remember about your *dream*."

His grip shifted on the wheel, and he turned us into the downtown district. "It's kind of foggy," he hedged. "You know how dreams get when you think about them."

"Well?" I prompted, and he frowned.

"I called 911. In my dream," he said, his neck muscles tight. "They told me to stay on the line, but I didn't. I ran down to see if you were all right. You were alone by the time I got to you, and you just sort of . . . went to sleep. Stopped breathing."

And I haven't had a real need to start up again since, I thought sourly. "Then what?" I didn't know what happened between my dying and the morgue. Barnabas wouldn't talk about it.

"Uh . . ." Josh kept his eyes on the road, looking nervous. "The ambulance got there before the cops. They put you in a black zipper bag. The sound of it going up . . . I'll never forget that." His posture shifted, and he seemed to be almost embarrassed. "The paramedics were really quiet when they lifted you out of the car. It was their job, but they were sad."

"I don't remember that part," I whispered. The guardian angel had gone back to her bell and was silently listening, her glow vanishing as soon as she landed.

"The cops . . ." Josh paused, pretending to look both ways as he collected himself. "They put me in the backseat, and they drove me to the hospital to get me checked out even though I said I hadn't been in the car. Then your dad was there. He was crying."

Guilt hunched me over. Ron said he had blocked this from my dad's memories, but how could he be sure? This was a nightmare.

"He said it wasn't my fault," Josh said, his voice low. "But I should've taken you home. And then the dream switches. Like nothing happened. I'm home cleaning the mud off my good shoes before my dad yells at me." I looked at him, and he shook his head while he watched the road. "And that's the weird thing, because I remember cleaning my shoes." He looked at his hands, then the road. "It was like it never happened and you were okay. I hate dreams like that."

I wondered how he could dismiss it as a dream, but I could see him trying to figure out where he had gotten mud on his shoes if he hadn't slid down a ravine after me.

"I ruined my dress," I said. "I'm still trying to pay for it."

Josh gave me a sideways look and shifted his grip on the wheel. "It was a *dream*. I mean, you're here. Alive."

I put my elbow on the open window and reached to touch the top. "Well, I'm here."

A scoffing noise came from him. "You're alive."

I fingered my amulet. "Not really." He stopped behind a gray Corvette, turning to me with a smile quirking his lips, and I said again, "Really, I'm not."

From Josh's Harley bell a tinkling voice said, "There once was a girl who wore Keds, who told everyone she was dead. Till they said she was hazy and labeled her crazy, and put her on all sorts of meds."

My bobbing foot—which was not wearing Keds—hit the bell, and the noise jerked Josh out of his reverie. "You know what?" he said as the Corvette and then his truck started moving again. "Forget I said anything. Man, everyone at school told me you were weird. I said you only needed someone to talk to, but damn, girl. You're whacked if you believe that, and if you don't, then you're really sad to be looking for attention by telling me you're dead."

I could understand why he didn't want to believe, but it still irritated me. "Well, let me fill in the gaps of your *dream*, okay?" I said tartly, giving up on keeping my angel in the dark. If Ron hadn't wanted her to know I had Kairos's amulet, he shouldn't have left her with me. "Kairos is dark, with a sexy accent that could make the lead singer of a girl band pee her pants. He kissed me. You remember that. I saw you."

"You kissed Kairos?" the guardian angel said, her already

high voice going thin and wondrous. "I don't even want to know what you did to get his amulet. Oh. My. God!"

That was insulting, and Josh saw me glare at the bell before he turned back to the road.

"Kairos held the door open for me when I got into his convertible," I continued. "You and Barnabas followed us out. Remember Barnabas? Tall guy with an annoyed expression? Anyway, the top was down." *The better to kill you with, my dear.*

The guardian angel laughed merrily. "Barnabas messed up your scythe prevention? Is that why he hasn't been working lately? Holy sweet seraph nubs. This gets better by the second!"

Josh was listening now too, and, encouraged, I continued, "The car goes off on the right side of the road," I said, going somber as I remembered it. "It flips twice. The windshield shatters on the first hit. I've got my seat belt on, so I don't get thrown out. It saved my life." I looked down at the belt around me now. *Old habits* . . . "When it's done rolling, Kairos is standing next to my door like nothing happened," I whispered, "and his nasty blade goes right through the car and me both. It leaves no blood. Not a mark."

The angel was on my knee, and a feeling of sympathy and warmth stole into me like a sunbeam. I gave her a smile, then looked up, tossing my hair from my eyes. "You left your car running. And you called my name twice as you ran down the hill." I felt sick remembering the fear in his voice. "I'm sorry, Josh. It wasn't your fault."

"Stop," he said. His hands gripped the wheel tight and he was breathing fast.

"He doesn't believe you," the angel said tartly.

"Would you have rather I let you keep believing it was a dream?" I protested.

Josh turned into the bike shop's lot, easing to a stop and putting his truck into park. "You are not dead."

I shrugged as I undid my seat belt. "They seemed to think so at the morgue."

Josh reached across the truck and jabbed a finger at me.

"Ow!" I yelped, drawing back and covering my upper arm as the angel giggled.

He smirked. "You're not dead. It's not funny anymore. Knock it off."

My pulse jumped into play, and I tried to stifle it. "It's the amulet. It gives me the illusion of a body." *And my memory of being alive supplies the rest,* I thought glumly.

"What amulet?" he asked, and I fished it out, holding it for his inspection. Josh's eyes widened, and I pulled it out of his reach, not wanting him to touch it.

"I swiped it from Kairos when he showed up at the morgue to claim my soul," I said, letting it thump back against me. "As long as I've got it, I'm fairly safe. But, uh, you aren't."

"Oh-h-h-h-h," the angel murmured. "Madison, you are in so

much trouble. I'm glad you're dead already. I don't think I could keep you alive if you weren't."

That made me feel tons better, and I scanned the sky for black wings. There was a haze of darker cloud in the distance. *Crows?*

"God, you're weird," Josh said as he turned off his truck and started to get out, the old metal creaking when he opened his door.

"You don't believe me?" I said, aghast. "After what I told you?" Ron was going to be royally P.O.'ed if I'd blown Josh's new memory for nothing. Not to mention he'd be mad at me for telling my guardian angel about the amulet. What did he expect, though? I was freaking dead. I think she would have figured it out eventually, first-sphere or not.

Josh was smiling as if it was a big joke. "I'll help you with your bike, Mad Madison. Can you get home from here?"

I stared at his empty seat when he got out, steaming from the nickname. I hated it. Hated it passionately. The first time I'd been sent to the principal's office it had been because I'd shoved a girl down for singing it. I'd been six, and it took most of my elementary school career to live it down.

My eyes closed in a long blink so I could find my temper, and I followed him. "Josh!" I exclaimed as I met him in back. "I'm not making this up. You know that's what happened! You were there!"

"It was a dream," he said as he put the tailgate down.

Frustrated, I put a fist on my hip. He didn't want it to be real, because if it was, he'd feel like it was his fault, like he should have insisted he take me home. "A dream that you keep having and I know all about?" I prompted, stepping back as the bike scraped across the liner.

"Sure," he said around a grunt as he lifted it free. "My mom would say it means I have a psychological hang-up about you. I'll get over it."

"You'll get dead!" I exclaimed, then lowered my voice as cars passed us not ten feet away. "Reapers can't find me, but they can find you."

"These are the guys with the scythes, right?" he asked, laughing.

I took my bike as he rolled it between us. "Josh, you were there the night I crashed. Kairos has seen you. He's looking for me, and he's going to use you to do it. The only reason you're safe right now is because you're with me."

He smiled, squinting in the sun. "A regular Wonder Woman, are you?"

"Stop laughing at me!" I said, imagining what was going to happen when school started back up. He and his friends were going to have a good laugh over this. If he survived. "It's the amulet that protects you, not me!" I couldn't tell him about my guardian angel. Not yet. He'd laugh his butt off.

His eyes flicked to the stone resting against my lower neck, and his amusement dimmed.

A black shadow ran over the parking lot and sent a spike of fear through me. I looked up to see a black wing. It kept moving, but there were three more across the street. This was so not good. In the ten seconds he'd been away from me, they'd gotten a whiff of him. "Just stay with me until Barnabas gets back, okay?"

"Barnabas?" he questioned, then shoved his tailgate up. "That's the guy from the prom."

"Yes." *Wings, amulet, can't miss him.*

His face was thoughtful as he took my bike from me and pushed it toward the shop.

"Look," I said, thinking he was starting to believe. "Do you see those things?"

I pointed to the slime-coated sheets of black slumped atop the post office's roof, and his smile quirked again. "The crows, Madison?"

I put a hand on my bike and stopped him from taking it inside. "They only look like crows, and I think the fact that you can see them at all means you've been marked." Susan had seen them yesterday too, from the boat. "They're called black wings. Reapers can use them to zero in on their victims. If you get too far from me, death is going to be knocking on your door." *And where the devil is my guardian angel?* I thought, suddenly realizing she was absent.

"Reapers," he said, chuckling, and I yanked the bike to a stop when he pushed it forward.

"Kairos knows your aura resonance. He can find you. Listen to me."

I wouldn't let him move the bike, and he suddenly shoved it back at me. "You are one weird chick, Madison."

"Josh, I'm serious!"

He didn't even turn around as he opened his truck door, saying over his shoulder, "What you are is seriously messed up. Don't talk to me, okay?"

A noise of frustration escaped me as he cranked his music and backed his truck up. His neck was red as he put it in gear, and after hesitating at the top of the entrance, he gunned the engine, tires spinning as he jerked his truck onto the road before traffic could trap him here with me.

"Idiot!" I exclaimed, then stiffened when, like lions scenting blood, all the black wings in sight lifted and turned. "Oh-h-h-h-h, crap," I whispered, spotting Josh sitting at a light half a block away. "Josh!" I shouted, but he couldn't hear me over his music.

The light changed, and he accelerated, clearly angry, by the way he was driving. My hand went to my mouth when a familiar black convertible appeared out of nowhere. It was Kairos. It had to be. And he was heading right for Josh.

A loud bang shook me, and a ball of electrical light flashed at the top of a pole. In a slow, majestic swoop, the traffic light swung to the pavement, the wire severed at the pole. Josh was right at the bottom of the arc.

"Josh!" I cried out, but he couldn't have heard me. He saw the light, though, and he slammed on the brakes, tires squealing as he swerved. Jumping the curb, he slid sideways into an ice-cream store's parking lot. Dust whirled up as he rocked to a halt. Behind him, the black convertible hit the falling traffic light in a spectacular bang of electricity, plastic, and metal. It was right where Josh would have been.

I dumped the bike and started running. A tall figure in black got out of the convertible, dressed formally, with luscious wavy black hair shining in the sun. I remembered his dusky skin, the scent of dead salt water on him. And his blue-gray eyes, looking distant and yet like they could see right through me. It was Kairos. My pace faltered at the stopped traffic. People were getting out of their cars.

The thump of Josh's truck door spiked adrenaline in me. "Hey, man! Are you okay?" he shouted as he jogged to Kairos.

"Josh," I whispered, too afraid to say it louder for fear Kairos would see me. Had Kairos made the traffic light fall to kill Josh, or had the light falling been a happy accident that saved him?

I ducked as a black wing swooped overhead, and my breath hissed in. Josh skidded to a halt in the middle of the road in front of Kairos. His face was pale, and he looked up as if he finally saw the dripping sheets of circling black for the first time. People were in my way, and I couldn't get to him. "Don't let him touch you!" I shouted, but it was too late.

My feet turned to clay as Kairos reached a thin hand out and gripped Josh's upper arm. The elegant man pulled him close, and it was as if I was watching my own death, reliving it. There was no scythe, but it wouldn't be hard to hide it, they were so close.

And then Josh jerked out of his reach. Stumbling, he warded Kairos off, continuing to put space between them as he backed away. He ducked as a black shape no one but the three of us could see dove at him.

Darting around the black convertible, I reached out and grabbed Josh's arm.

"Hey!" he shouted, pulling out of my grip; then he recognized me. His glasses were askew, and his blue eyes had fear in them, fear that he finally believed me and fear that death was standing in the intersection—looking at us.

Terror seized my muscles. People were between us and Kairos, asking him if he was okay. Someone jostled me, and, startled, I tugged Josh backward, my eyes never leaving Kairos. *He had wanted me dead even before I stole his amulet. Why?* "Come on," I said, pulling Josh into the press of people. "Get in your truck!"

I jumped when my guardian angel's laughter tinkled nearby. "There once was a boy full of class," the light sang, "who always skipped his Sunday mass. He almost hit death, but missed Kairos Seth. He'll never know who saved his ass."

"Get in the truck!" I shouted, tugging at Josh, who was still staring at Kairos. I didn't think the black wings could see us now because my guardian angel was back. She was probably the one who had made the light fall, causing Josh to swerve out of the way and Kairos to crash, thereby attracting enough attention so that the dark timekeeper couldn't easily kill him.

"It's him," Josh said, pale as he fixed his glasses back on his nose. "He asked about you," he added, and I pushed him through the rubbernecking crowd to his truck, his music still blaring and adding to the confusion.

"Wow, big surprise," I muttered. I could hear a siren, and I sent a grateful look in the direction of my guardian angel. She'd stopped Kairos in such a way that Josh had been a bystander. Not a scratch on his car nor a reason for us to stick around. Kairos, though, would have a hard time leaving, buying us more time to get away. She was good. No, she was great!

The hot sun was bouncing up from the ice-cream store's parking lot when I yanked Josh's truck door open. "Don't Fear the Reaper" was blasting out, and I slid across the seat and pulled Josh in after me. My guardian angel was singing, her tinkling voice adding to the travesty.

"The truck moves, right?" I said, and Josh took a deep breath. Hands shaking, he put the truck, still running, in gear. Carefully edging back into the street, he accelerated. Every second put more space between Josh and Kairos, between Kairos and me.

Josh turned his music off, much to the guardian angel's disappointment. His gaze was behind us more than in front. In a flurry of panicked motion, he put his seat belt on.

"Are you okay?" I asked, then leaned in to look at his speed-ometer. I'd never seen someone as white as he was now. Maybe I should have been driving.

He licked his lips. "That was him. He asked for you by name."

My chest hurt, and I took a deep breath to explain. "At least he didn't kill you. Hey, can you slow down? There are other people here."

"He might follow us," he said. I put a comforting hand on his arm, but it made him jump.

"He can't track you by your aura because of my amulet—as long as you are close to me, you're safe."

From the bell came a voice chiming, "It's the angel, baby, not your amulet."

"Yeah," I shot back, "but he won't believe that."

Crap. I closed my mouth and cringed. Josh slowed down as a cop car raced past us, heading for the accident. Pulling to the curb, he turned to me. "Who are you talking to? Please, please, please don't tell me it's dead people."

My head started to hurt. I was really stupid sometimes. "Uh, my, uh, guardian angel," I said hesitantly. "She's, uh, on your Harley bell."

"Guardian angel?"

I gave him a sickly smile. "She's a Guardian, Reaper-Augmented

Cherub, Extinction Security, one-seventy-six. Or G.R.A.C.E.S. one-seventy-six for short." I couldn't call her that. Grace, though, maybe.

Josh began to protest, and Grace made the bell *ping*. Josh stared at it, white-faced. "Madison?" he said softly.

"Yes?"

"You're dead?"

I nodded. "Yup."

He swallowed, both hands on the wheel as he looked up through the strip of blue-tinted glass to the sky. "And those aren't crows?"

Wincing, I noted the black wings were at the horizon again, circling. "No," I said, and Josh let his forehead hit the steering wheel with a soft *thump*.

"But you're okay?" he said to his knees.

"Because I have my amulet," I said, holding it. "You're okay because Ron left me with a guardian angel while he tries to convince the seraphs to let me keep it." Twisting, I turned to look behind us. "Kairos knows your aura resonance from the prom, but he can't see it if you're with me. But maybe we should, uh, get moving again."

Not saying a word, Josh checked behind him and put the truck back in gear. We headed through town by way of the side roads. "Uh," I said uncertainly, "you want to come over to my house for a sandwich?"

"S-sure."

I licked my lips, not liking his shell-shocked expression as he made a left to get on the interstate and take the long way to the other side of town. I knew how it felt to have death touch you, realizing you'd be dead but for the whim of something that really didn't care one way or the other.

"I'm sorry you got involved," I said, remembering Josh's voice when he slid down the slope that night, trying to reach me even as Kairos cut my thread of life. "You were there. It wasn't a dream. But I want to thank you. Because of you, I didn't die alone."

Five

Josh sat uneasily at the rectangular table in the kitchen, his legs stretching from one end to the other. He had made two sandwiches for himself, and the shaved ham spilled out all over. He liked ice in his pop, and barbecue-flavored chips. Me, I had a thin sandwich, a handful of chips, and a glass of iced tea. I enviously watched him slam down half his soda in one gulp. I hadn't been hungry since I'd hit ctrl/alt/del. Coming up with excuses for my dad as to why I wasn't eating was getting harder.

The kitchen hadn't been remodeled since the house was built, and the white-and-yellow-tiled splashboard and the cream-colored walls looked tired. The cupboards were a blah brown, and the fridge was the one I remembered from before my parents separated. But tucked in a corner was a state-of-the-art coffee-maker, proving my dad had his priorities. There was a small lazy Susan with napkins, salt and pepper, and a dusty ashtray sitting right where it would be in my mom's kitchen—whispers of her still in my dad's life though she'd been gone for years.

Josh looked at my sandwich as I sat across from him. "Is that all you're going to eat?" he questioned, and I shrugged.

"I don't sleep much, either," I said as I fingered a chip and wondered if Grace, currently singing limericks in the light fixture, ate anything. Barnabas didn't. "Late-night TV gets old after a few months."

Late-night TV, uninterrupted Internet surfing, staring at the ceiling when Barnabas was through with me . . . not much fun when you had no one to share it with. The info on auras I'd gotten off the Internet hadn't helped. Neither had the stuff on angels. Barnabas had laughed so hard he'd almost rolled off the roof when I'd brought out my laptop to show him before our nightly—and apparently useless—attempts at teaching me how to touch thoughts. *I've been failing because I have Kairos's amulet?* I thought, fingering it. Maybe it was like trying to get a U.S. hair dryer to work in a British socket.

"So you're dead," Josh said around his full mouth.

The iced tea made my teeth ache, and I glanced at the clock. *It's been hours. Where are they?* "Yup."

"And that amulet gives you a body," he prompted.

"The solid illusion of one, yes," I said, fidgeting. "It also hides me from the black wings so they don't suck my soul away. A soul without a body is fair game. That's why they anticipate reaps, hoping to snitch some. They don't show up at normal deaths—just when you've been marked early." I pulled the crusts off my sandwich, but I didn't have it in me to eat it.

He eyed the mutilated crust. "Keep your amulet on, 'kay? Black wings give me the creeps."

"Not a problem." *I should have practiced more,* I thought. Then again, if I had a dark timekeeper stone, my aura resonance would shift far from Barnabas's when I tried to use it. More like Nakita's. *Maybe I could touch thoughts with Nakita?*

"So . . ." Josh said hesitantly, bringing my wandering thoughts back. "Where's your real one? Body, I mean." His brow pinched. "You didn't bury it in the backyard, did you?"

"Kairos has it," I admitted, a sliver of fear flickering through me. "At least, he stole it out of the morgue when I . . . ran."

Josh shifted his feet and bumped my chair leg. "That's ugly. Kairos was that guy in the black car, right? He's a reaper?"

I winced, not wanting to tell him he was a keeper of time. It sounded so lame. "He's actually the dark reapers' head guy," I said, thinking that was marginally better. "Barnabas is a light reaper. He tries to save the people that the dark reapers target."

Josh took another bite and wiped the corner of his mouth. "Like you?"

"Yes, but he messed up because it was my birthday." Fidgeting, I rearranged the chips on my plate. "He thought Kairos was going after you, actually."

His chewing slowed as his eyebrows rose. "I didn't know it

was your birthday. No wonder you were all pissy. Set up by your dad on your birthday? That's wrong."

I smiled a lopsided smile, and he smiled back. From the light fixture, Grace giggled.

My eyes dropped, and Josh went back to his sandwich. "I sort of remember Barnabas. You said he can keep those things from getting me? Where is he? Uh . . . heaven?"

I shook my head. "He's with Ron, his boss." Tension was winding tighter in me as we sat and did nothing. *Why am I playing tea party with Josh when death is looking for us?* Brushing my bangs back, I gazed out the kitchen window to the empty street. "Kairos wants his amulet back. Ron thinks I should keep it." *What if they never show up?*

"But Kairos has an amulet," Josh said. "I saw it."

Smiling grimly, I nodded. "Apparently it's not as powerful as the one I took. As bad as I feel for him, I'd rather stay alive, thank you. He shouldn't have killed me in the first place," I muttered.

His expression thoughtful, Josh propped his elbows on the table. "Kairos came back for your soul at the morgue. That's messed up."

"Yeah," I said, stifling a shudder. "He targeted me, killed me, then came back for me. They never do that." *Why me? I'm not special.*

"So you're a reaper now?" Josh said, looking uncomfortable. "Like in the books where if you cheat death, you take his place?"

"No freaking way!" I exclaimed. "Only a reaper can be a reaper. I'm just dead."

That seemed to give Josh a measure of peace as he settled back and started on his second sandwich. "This is so weird."

I snorted and ate a chip. "You have no idea," I said, then slid my sandwich to him, minus the crusts, which I picked at. Though I was upset, it was nice having someone to talk shop with besides Barnabas. I should've done this months ago. Not that Josh would have believed me, much less talked to me. I'd been spending so much time in my room e-mailing Wendy about nothing that I hadn't tried to make any new friends. *Maybe I should change that*, I thought sadly. That is, if I survived. Where in God's creation was Barnabas?

Josh began chuckling, and I eyed him. "I'm kind of glad you're dead."

"Why?" I asked, miffed. "So you can eat my lunch?"

Elbows on the table, he smiled. "Because it means I'm not crazy."

My brief smile faded. "I'm sorry. You weren't supposed to remember anything. It must have been awful, having a memory like that when everything is telling you it's a dream. Is it bad? I think my dad remembers stuff too." Me in the morgue, the call never completed to my mom. The guilt, the loss . . . boxes to be filled, taped up, and put in the attic.

His eyes down, Josh nodded. I heard a car pull into the drive and got up. It was my dad, and after seeing Josh's truck, he backed out and parked in the street so he didn't block him in. "What's my dad doing home?" My attention shifted to the clock on the stove. It was only one thirty.

Wiping the chip crumbs off himself, Josh shifted in his seat. "You don't think he heard about what happened, do you? I probably shouldn't have driven off like that."

My dad was eyeing Josh's truck as he came up the walk, squinting until he found the shade. His khakis and dress shirt made him look professional, but he was still wearing his lab coat—which meant I was in trouble. He never forgot to take it off unless he was upset. His work ID dangled from around his neck, and he tucked it into the lab coat's breast pocket when he reached the drive.

"We didn't do anything wrong by leaving," I said, suddenly nervous. "It wasn't your fault Kairos hit a traffic light. You didn't hit anything."

"It was my fault!" Grace chimed out, and the light fixture she was in glowed brighter.

"I was a witness." Josh pulled a phone from his pocket and looked at it.

"How would he find out, though?" I muttered, pulling back from the window when my dad looked up at the house.

Josh shifted his glass so it was perfectly situated with his plate. "It's a small town," he said, his brow pinched in worry. "I should call my mom."

We both stiffened when the front door opened. "Madison?"

my dad's voice echoed in the silent house. "Are you home?"

I gave Josh a nervous look. "We're in the kitchen, Dad."

His shoes thumped on the hardwood floor, and he appeared in the archway to the hall. Josh stood, and my dad's eyebrows rose as he took him in. "Hello, sir," Josh said, extending his hand. "I'm Josh Daniels."

My dad's puzzled expression eased and turned into one of acceptance. "Oh! Mark's son. You look just like him. It's good to meet you." His grip pulled away. "You're the one who left Madison at the prom," he accused in a defensive-dad sort of way.

"Dad!" I protested, embarrassed. "He didn't leave me. I ran out on him after I realized you set us up. Josh was a perfect gentleman. I asked him over to lunch to try to make up for it."

Josh was shifting from foot to foot, but my dad had found his usual good humor, and his face showed a smile again. "I thought maybe it was because your bike had a flat and you needed a ride somewhere," he said, his eyebrows arched.

I blinked. "H-how did you know?" I stammered.

My dad put a hand on my shoulder and gave it a quick squeeze before he went to the message machine. "I got a call from the bike shop."

My mouth opened into an O as I remembered I'd left it there. "Oh. Yeah. About that—"

"They ran the registration number and came up with my name," my dad said as he turned away from the machine and frowned. "Why didn't you answer your phone? I've been trying to reach you for an hour. Even called the Flower Bower to see if you went in on your day off. I finally had to leave work."

Embarrassed, I shrugged. I hadn't checked my phone in all the commotion today. "Uh. Sorry. I ran out of minutes," I lied. "Josh gave me a ride." My dad's frown was making me nervous. "So I asked him for lunch." Crap, I was babbling, and I shut my mouth.

A soft sound of disapproval escaped him. "Can I talk to you for a moment?" he said dryly, passing through the second archway to the never-used dining room.

I sighed. "Excuse me," I said to Josh, then glumly followed my dad. He had gone all the way through the dining room and was standing in the patch of sun that made it into the living room, shining on the wall where he'd hung some of the photos I'd taken at the balloon festival with him last month. He'd sprung for a ride in one, and you could see the entire old downtown in one shot, the rivers outlining its confines.

The living room, like the kitchen, held whispers of my mom, from the glass-topped tables to the suede furniture to the Art Deco statue in the corner. Either my parents had very similar decorating ideas, or my dad was still living in the past, surrounding himself with reminders of her. No pictures of her, though.

"Dad—" I started, but he didn't give me a chance to explain.

"Stop," he said, hand raised. "What did we agree on about guests?"

I took a breath to speak and let it out. "I'm sorry. But it's Josh. You set me up with him, so I thought it'd be okay. It's just a sandwich." My voice had gotten whiny, and I hated it.

"It's not the sandwich; it's you being here alone with him."

"Da-a-a-a-ad," I moaned, "I'm seventeen."

His eyebrows went up. "What's the agreement?" he asked, and I slumped.

"I said I'd ask before inviting people over," I mumbled. "I'm sorry. I forgot."

Immediately he relented and gave me a sideways hug. My dad couldn't stay mad at me, especially when it appeared I was starting to make some friends. "It looks like you forgot a lot," he said when he let go. "Like your bike? Madison, that bike wasn't cheap. I can't believe you left it there."

If he was talking money, then we were cool. "Sorry," I hedged as I tried to get him to go back to the kitchen. "Josh almost got into an accident and I got distracted."

At the word *accident*, my dad pulled me around. "Are you okay?" he gasped as he held my upper arms and gave me a once-over.

"Dad, it's okay," I said, and his grip dropped. "I wasn't even in the car. A traffic light fell, and Josh swerved out of the way." Kairos could stay out of the story.

"Madison," he began, looking scared, and a memory surfaced

of me finding him alone in my room, surrounded by packing boxes and believing I was dead.

"Not a scratch or anything," I said, to get that awful picture out of my own head. "It was the other guy who hit the traffic light."

My dad searched my face to see if I was telling the truth. "You mean a stop sign," he said, and I shook my head.

"Traffic light," I affirmed, finding the humor in it as Grace laughed from the kitchen. "It fell right off the wire and some guy ran into it. If it hadn't, he might have hit Josh instead."

Finally he lost that frightened look. Pulling himself straight, he exhaled. "Sounds like his guardian angel was working overtime."

A glowing ball of light zipped into the room. "You got that right, baby cakes," Grace said, her glow lost as she hovered in a sunbeam. "I'm not even supposed to be guarding him, but Madison's not nice to me, and he is. Gave me a bell to sit in and everything."

I glanced at her voice, seeing the backyard behind her and the hedge that Mrs. Walsh somehow saw around, over, or through. "He's really a good driver, Dad," I said. "Wears his seat belt and everything."

My dad laughed, his hand landing on my shoulder again before it dropped away. "I know your mother gave you a lot more freedom—"

"Not really," I interrupted, recalling her strict rules and early curfews, demands that I be proper and respectable like her when all I wanted to do was be myself.

"Call me next time you want to have friends over, okay?"

He turned me around, and together we started back to the kitchen. "I'm sorry; I will." I'd apologized, stated my case without whining—much—and he'd accepted that. I was getting better at this responsibility thing.

"Did you get enough to eat?" he said as we entered the kitchen, and I nodded.

Josh was on his cell phone, and seeing us, he said, "Bye," and closed it. I had a moment of worry that he might be talking to his buddies about that "weird chick Madison," but then dismissed it when he smiled at me. Cripes, he had a nice smile. Better yet, he believed me. It was as if a weight had been lifted. I wasn't alone anymore.

"Thanks for bringing Madison home," my dad said, and I felt better. He liked him, too.

Josh seemed to get that I wasn't in trouble, and he found a more relaxed position. "It wasn't a problem," he said, fiddling with his glass. "Right on the way home."

"On the way home from what?" my dad asked as he got the iced tea out of the fridge.

I hesitated. I hadn't told my dad I was going to the school today.

"School," Josh said, adjusting his glasses and clearly curious to hear the excuse I was going to give my dad for being there.

"The track team is running tomorrow at the carnival, so we had a practice. Would you like to sponsor me? It's a dollar per circuit."

"Sure. Put me down," he said, hunched over as he rummaged in the dishwasher for a glass. I winced, remembering I was supposed to empty it this morning. "You're not a long-distance runner, are you?" he asked with mild worry, clearly thinking big bucks out of his wallet.

"No. I'm a miler."

My dad smiled as he poured his tea. I was starting to wish he would go away. I had things to do. People to save.

"Madison, you didn't tell me you were going to do anything for the carnival."

"Uh . . ." I scrambled for an answer, thinking. "I thought I could, uh, take pictures. But it's a stupid idea."

"No it's not," Josh said, and I could've smacked him. "People love that kind of stuff."

I gave him a look that said to shut up, then smiled when my dad turned from closing the fridge. "Who'd pay for a picture they can't see and won't get until two days later?" I protested.

My dad was nodding, but not in agreement with me. I'd seen that thoughtful expression on him before, and he leaned against the counter with his drink and crossed his ankles. "If that's all you need, I'll get you one of those printers that lets you do it right there," he said, and my stomach dropped. "You give them a ticket, and they pick it up before they leave."

"Really?" I said with forced enthusiasm. Maybe I could call my boss at the flower shop and offer to come in tomorrow to get out of it.

"Sure," he said, then shoved his glasses back up his nose. "I almost got you one for your birthday, but I wanted you to have a better camera first."

I thought of my new camera up on my dresser, used mostly for taking shots of my flashy new wardrobe my dad had gotten me and e-mailing them to Wendy. She'd probably die when she saw the picture of my skull-and-crossbones sneakers. "Thanks, Dad," I said, giving him a pained look, trying to tell him I wanted to be alone with Josh. "I'll talk to someone about it."

"You do that." Giving us a salute with his glass, he ambled toward the archway. "Josh, you're welcome to stay for dinner if you want."

"Thanks, Mr. A.," Josh said, "but I told my mom I'd be home by six thirty."

My dad bobbed his head in acknowledgment, smiling at the informal term of respect. I was sure he'd never been called that before. Barnabas was always very formal the few times he'd talked to my dad. "I'll be in my office," my dad said. "I've got a few things to finish up for today, but I can do them from home."

I sighed as he left the kitchen. I could hear his footsteps in the entryway, and the creak of his office door not quite shutting. He didn't do much work at his home office, but it was right across from the kitchen, and he could keep an ear on us.

"There once was a girl from Zaire—"

"Please don't," I moaned softly, and Grace snickered. Maybe I could find a bell for her to live in. Seeing that traffic light crash down had been scary.

"He doesn't trust me," I said softly as I sat across from Josh. *Six thirty?* We had almost five hours for Barnabas to turn up and make this nightmare go away. Where was he anyway? It couldn't take that long to talk to seraphs. Just drop to your knees and have at it.

Josh snorted and ate another chip. "He doesn't trust *me*, that's who he doesn't trust."

I smiled thinly, elbows on the table as my dad talked on the phone. Black wings didn't clock out at the end of business hours, and if Barnabas wasn't back by then, it was going to get ugly. It had been a while since I'd been grounded for breaking curfew, but if I didn't stay with Josh all night, he might not make it. It wasn't as if Grace could play messenger girl.

"I don't suppose you have any ideas about how to keep Kairos away after six thirty?" Josh asked, and I gave him an apologetic look.

"Nothing that won't get me grounded." I glanced at Grace, knowing the only way she'd leave to get Ron would be if I was in danger that she couldn't handle, and in that case, I'd probably be dead. *This is so not good.* "One of them should be back by now. Maybe something's wrong."

From the light, Grace chimed out, "Nothing's wrong. If you aren't allowed past heaven's gates, it takes a while to get a seraph's attention."

"I feel so helpless!" I said, collapsing in my chair again.

"Helpless? You want to talk helpless?" Grace grumbled, her thin voice growing louder as she landed on the table. "I don't even know why I'm here. Barnabas can do a better job guarding you than I can. Why Ron twitched him away instead of asking another reaper's help to talk to the seraphs is beyond me."

"You're doing a great job," I said, giving Josh an eye-rolling look when he stared at me, hearing only half the conversation. "You scared the crap out of me when you sent that light down on Kairos. That had to be second-sphere stuff, easy."

Josh smiled and finished off his sandwich. "Scared the crap out of me, too. Thanks for saving my life."

The glow from her wings brightened. "It was clever, wasn't it?"

I nodded as I stood up, gathering the empty plates and taking them to the sink. Why *had* Ron taken Barnabas with him? It was almost as if he didn't want the reaper with me anymore.

Ice sloshed as Josh took a drink, and he reddened as he wiped his chin. "I don't want to get grounded," he said. "There has to be something we can do between now and six thirty."

"You mean like come up with a plan to get rid of Kairos?" I asked as I rinsed the plates off. "Sure, like I can take on the king of the dark reapers," I said, but then I thought about it. "Actually, that's not a bad idea," I admitted, drying my fingers off. "If

I swiped his new amulet, he couldn't tap into the time stream until he made a new one. He'd have to leave. He wouldn't have a scythe then, either."

Josh's expression was puzzled when I turned around. "Can't he just borrow one of his reapers' amulets?"

I smiled, realizing I'd said "time stream," and Josh was still sitting there listening to me. "No. Kairos can touch a reaper's amulet," I said, remembering Ron holding Barnabas's, "but not use it. Neither can Ron." I went silent, holding my amulet as I remembered Nakita's stone glowing the same shade as the jewel on her sword. "My getting close to him probably isn't a good idea. He'll just drag me off. And if you try to take it, he'll just scythe you. There's got to be a way to make this work."

My foot started to jiggle, but Josh calmly pushed his glasses up and ate a chip. I could tell he felt guilty about being afraid, but we were talking about walking death, and in no way was it even his problem. It was mine.

"You can't use a reaper's amulet, but you can use Kairos's?" he said despite his full mouth. "What makes his so special?"

"Uh, because Kairos's amulet isn't really a reaper's stone," I said hesitantly. "It's a timekeeper's," I added, emboldened by his acceptance of the "time stream" comment. "And timekeepers are human. I guess they dilute the divine or something for them."

"Timekeeper," Josh said softly, and, apparently satisfied, he went back to the chips. "You were lucky you didn't take a reaper's amulet by mistake."

"Yeah, lucky," I said, feeling uneasy. That Kairos had come back for my soul was creepy enough, but why had he targeted me? How would my being dead move him to a "higher court," as he had said the night he'd killed me? Was I fated to do something so horribly wrong that it endangered angels?

"Maybe just being human isn't enough to use this thing, and that's why I can't do anything with it," I said morosely as I swung my amulet, and Josh perked up.

"Well, what should you be able to do with it?"

Blowing my purple bangs from my eyes, I thought about it. If it was a timekeeper's amulet, I might be able to do what Ron could—in theory. "Besides thought-touch with a reaper? Um, I guess I should be able to stop small chunks of time," I said, remembering the shifting shadows when Ron showed up or left. "Or go misty—kind of ghostlike. I've seen him do that. Change memories. Ron changed my amulet's resonance twice, now. Barnabas can shrink an amulet's influence down so it doesn't interfere with black wings smelling out a victim and Barnabas can use amulets to find the target, so I'm assuming a timekeeper can do the same. And he said something once about laying down a fake trail for the black wings to trick the dark reapers who follow them for the same reason."

My gaze dropped to the table. "Barnabas says I might not be able to touch thoughts with him because my amulet used to belong to a dark timekeeper and he's a light reaper. Polar opposites. The only thing I've tried to do is thought-touching."

Josh leaned back with his arms over his chest. "Well, there you go. You should try something else. Something that doesn't have anything to do with reapers. If you could go misty, you could walk up to him and just *pftt*. His new amulet would be yours."

I stared at him, considering it. Stealing Kairos's new amulet might very well be that easy. Smiling at Josh, I felt like I had hope again—a reason to try. "Will you help me?"

From the light fixture, Grace murmured, "I don't like this," which perversely made me feel even more hopeful.

"Absolutely!" Josh's enthusiasm made me think he wasn't eager to sleep in his closet tonight, hiding from the dark reaper. Who could blame him, though?

Smiling, I stood, chair scraping. "Come on. Let's get out of here."

"Why?"

I cocked my head toward the other end of the house. "I'm not going to practice when my dad is around." I knew my dad wouldn't let me entertain in my room, but there had to be some-where public we could go where no one would look twice at us. Maybe the library. I'd snuck in there a couple of times at night after I caught the librarian hiding the key behind a brick. I was starting to like this small town.

"But . . ." he said slowly, worry pinching his eyes.

"You'll be fine," I moaned, dragging him up out of his chair.

"The guardian angel goes where I do. You're covered. We've only got till six thirty. Do you want to trust that Barnabas will show between now and then?"

Nodding, Josh took his glass to the sink. "Okay."

Excitement raced down to my toes. "Dad?" I called loudly. "Josh and I are going into town to get an extra card for my camera. Okay?"

"Take your phone," his voice came filtering back. "Buy more minutes. Be back by six."

"Got it!" I slapped my hand to the back pocket of my shorts to feel the bump of my phone. I turned to Josh, really glad he had a set of wheels. "Ready to go?"

He looked at me, bemused. "Where? My house is out. My mom works from home."

There was a little tinkling laugh from above me somewhere. "There once was a girl who liked lying, who only got worse after dying."

"The library?" I said. "But can we go to the mall first? I really do have to pick up a new memory card. Since I'm playing photographer at the carnival now. Thanks," I finished dryly.

Josh grinned. "If I'm still alive tomorrow morning, do you want a ride?"

"You know it," I said, smiling. He wanted to pick me up, and I didn't think it was just because of the black wings. I think he liked me.

I waved bye to my dad when he rolled his desk chair to his

office door to see us leave, giving me a smile. I couldn't help but feel good. It wasn't simply that Josh might like me, either. I'd been banging my head against a wall for months trying to use my amulet, feeling more and more stupid as Barnabas got more and more despondent. If I could figure this out with Josh, then I wouldn't have to rely on Barnabas or Ron so much. I could do this on my own.

Well, I mused as Josh closed the door behind me and searched his pockets for his keys, maybe not entirely alone, but I was going to do it.

Six

I'd only been to The Lowest Common Denominator, or the Low D as everyone called it, once before. My dad had taken me for pizza, and the casual eatery had been packed with college students either cramming for finals or relaxing after theirs were done. I knew he'd been trying to help me fit in, but pizza with my dad when everyone else was on their own hadn't painted the picture I'd been hoping to make. Maybe if I'd been able to go invisible that night, I might have had more luck making friends.

Smiling at the thought, I picked at a French fry. Josh was hungry again—or still, maybe—which was how a quick pit stop here had made it a convenient place to practice, seeing as the large hangout was nearly empty. That had been almost an hour ago, and I was starting to get anxious. Maybe it wasn't the amulet, as Barnabas had said. Maybe it really was me. I'd seen a black wing drift through the parking lot when Josh had gone to the little boys' room, and the panicked face I'd made trying to reach Barnabas's thoughts had put Grace into stitches.

We'd already been to the mall, and there was a new photo card in the trendy bag on the table, right beside my untouched soda and the fries. It was Josh's second plate, and he ate with a steady pace as he dipped fries in spicy cheese and watched me for signs of "ghosting," as he called it.

Afternoon light streamed in through the big plate-glass windows that looked out on the mall. Low D had once been a burger joint, but bowing to convention, they now served lattes and had free wi-fi access. There was a center space with coffee tables and cushioned chairs, and booths around the edges. A few people were plugged in, hunched over their laptops, and eating overpriced sandwiches and gourmet kettle chips as they surfed.

Lonely arcade sounds filtered out from the dark cave set to one side as the machines talked to themselves. Coming from the attached skate arena was the rumble of wheels where skaters tried their nerve and their boards on artificial hills and railings in the "snake pit." The sound of skateboards on plywood rose up through me like a second pulse of blood. Grace was at the register, resting in the bell that supposedly rang when someone in the snake pit jumped high enough to trigger it. One of the walls was a thick, scuff-marked sheet of Plexiglas, and hazy images moved beyond it in time with the rumbling.

I turned from the transparent wall and my gaze went back to Josh. My fingers were tingling, but I thought it was because I was gripping my amulet too tightly, not because I was close to figuring this thing out. Perhaps I'd been too optimistic thinking I could learn how to do something useful in so short a time, but I was tired of relying on someone else for my safety, and Josh had been willing to help. "Can you see me now?" I asked hopefully.

Josh's eyes met mine squarely, and I slumped. "I think you're trying too hard," he said.

Slowly I let go of my amulet. "We've only got a few hours left. It's not like this thing came with an instruction manual." Depressed, I ran my fingers over my wax-and-paper cup to wipe the condensation off. Barnabas had been less than helpful the time I'd asked him about it after a particularly frustrating night. He'd only said he "thought slippery thoughts" and that I'd better spend my time learning how to contact him if I needed help. Slippery thoughts. Yeah, and if I thought happy thoughts, I'd sprout wings and fly.

"You've only been at it for an hour. Don't be so hard on yourself. We've got a little time yet," Josh said, but his eyes were squinting in worry.

Time, I thought as I wadded my straw wrapper into a ball and dropped it. Maybe I should have tried to learn how to slow time, but that sounded way harder than going invisible.

"Don't worry about it," Josh said, but I could tell he was getting nervous. Meeting death was not something you could easily shake off, and the memory of Kairos standing in the moonlight with his scythe bared as I sat helpless in a smashed-up convertible drifted through me.

My hand went back to my amulet, and I held the stone, seeking assurance that even if it was a dark timekeeper's amulet, I was here and sort of alive. Waking up in the morgue and seeing myself on the table had been the single most frightening thing in my life. Even worse, I knew it was my fault for having gotten into his car to begin with, mega-cuteness aside. Kairos wasn't so cute anymore. I couldn't believe I'd kissed him.

I gripped the amulet harder. It had been with me for months now, the weight of it familiar and comforting. Without it, I wouldn't only be invisible, but insubstantial, able to pass through walls and closed doors. Black wing bait. Ghostlike. Maybe that was the key to it all. Not thinking slippery thoughts, but sort of finding a way to block the stone's influence.

Staring at the table, I sifted through my thoughts for the memory of that awful moment in the morgue. I'd been able to feel my heartbeat and the air move in my lungs as I breathed from reflex, but my body had been in the black body bag, unable to sense the coldness of the granite or the smoothness of the plastic surrounding it. I'd been divorced from it. The tie to my body had been broken. It just hadn't been there. And, scared, I'd run.

When I'd fled, the air had grown thin in me, like I was

becoming as insubstantial as it was—almost equalizing. My knees had gone wobbly. The touch of real objects had hurt, as if grating upon my bone. It was only after Barnabas had come after me that I'd felt normal again. Only then had I been in a position to understand and recognize what I'd lost. With the lack of a body, the universe hadn't recognized me. That is, until Barnabas's amulet got close enough and it had something to grab on to again and bring me back in line with everything else.

Perhaps with the separation from my body, I'd lost what time and the universe used to pull me forward. Maybe the amulets were like artificial points that time and the universe could fasten onto and use to keep mind and soul in sync with the present. And if I could break those ties . . .

Anxious, I squirmed on the hard seat, believing I was on the right track. Eyes still closed, I fell deep into my thoughts and tried to see myself as a singular identity, tied to the present by the threads of the past. I could hear the noise around me: Josh slurping his drink, the jingle of the store's phone—and after months of learning how to concentrate, something finally went my way.

Excitement shot through me as I suddenly could see the line my life had made. Tense, I saw how I grew from a possibility to a presence, marveling at how my life wove in and out of other people's lives, and then the ugly snarl where I'd died, almost as if time or space were making a knot to hold itself together when a soul was cut out of it. It was as if the memory of others bound the darkness here where I'd left it, giving it shape by what was lacking, a ghost of a presence that burst suddenly back into existence when I had obtained an amulet. But now, time wasn't using my body to find my soul and carry it forward; it was using the amulet I had swiped from Kairos. The color, or maybe the sound, was different. It had been a dark blue up to the point when I had died, and then, an abrupt shift to a purple so black it had a tinge of ultraviolet in it. Like Nakita's.

My aura, I realized, wanting to drop everything and try to touch Barnabas's thoughts, but I brought my attention back. I felt myself shiver when I realized I could see my soul throwing lines of thought into the future—for thought must have to move faster than time. I could actually see the violet-colored lines extending from me into the future, pulling me on with the rest of the universe. What made it all work, what colored the lines from my death onward, was the amulet giving time something on which to fasten.

And if I could break some of those lines running from the amulet to the present, maybe I'd become invisible, like I'd been when I'd run from Barnabas in the morgue. Almost as if I wasn't wearing the stone even though it remained about my neck.

Anticipation made me shiver, and I unfocused enough of my attention to make sure I was still sitting with Josh and nothing was going on. This had to work. We were running out of time. I wouldn't destroy all the threads—just a few—and none of the lines that were pulling me into the future. Just the ones that tied me to this instant of right-this-second.

I took a slow breath that I didn't need, and as I exhaled, I plucked a thread that held me to the present. It separated like spider silk, making a soft hum of sound in my mind as it parted. Encouraged, I ran a theoretical hand between me and the present, taking out a larger swath. The rumbling from the snake pit seemed to echo through me. I could almost see the sound coming in waves in my imagination, passing through me to bounce against the far side of the booth.

"Madison?" Josh whispered, and my eyes flew open. I stared at the table, my fingers tingling. "It's working," he said, awe in his voice.

I inhaled as if coming up from deep water. My head snapped up and I stared at him. The sound of the skaters became real again, the imagined waves of sound gone but for in my thoughts. My heart pounded, and I felt dizzy, almost as if I was alive. Josh was staring at me, his blue eyes wide.

"It worked!" he said again, leaning forward over his fries. "You're back now, but I could see the seat behind you!" He glanced around to see if anyone had noticed. "It was the weirdest thing I've ever seen. Do it again," he prompted.

Relief filled me, and I shifted on the stiff cushion. "Okay. Here goes."

Nervous and excited, I settled myself with my palms flat on the table as I willed it to happen again. Eyes open, I stared at the sky visible through the front windows. My focus blurred, and I fell into my thoughts. I felt the stone's presence everywhere in my recent past, weaving a net to tie each moment of time to the next. It was easier now, and with a finger of thought, I touched the new violet web that had formed and made it shrivel and fall away. The sounds around me grew hollow and I felt the queasy sensation of going insubstantial. The thudding of my heart, even if it was only a memory, vanished.

"Holy smokes, Madison!" Josh exclaimed in a hushed rush of words. "You're gone!" He hesitated. "Are you . . . there? I don't believe this."

I concentrated, breaking a good number of threads as they shifted from the future to the present, making sure to leave enough to pull me forward. "I'm here," I said, feeling my lips move and hearing my words as if from far away. I brought my gaze to Josh, finding it easier with practice. His eyes were roving everywhere, focusing mostly on the seat behind me.

"Sweet," he said as he drew back. "I can hardly hear you. You sound creepy. Like you're whispering into a phone or something."

A tight hum at my ear told me Grace had abandoned the bell by the register. I turned to the bright light darting frantically about the booth, and my mouth dropped open. "I can see you," I whispered. "My God, you're beautiful." She was only a minute tall, even though her glow made her look softball-sized. Her complexion was dark and her facial features were delicately sharp. Gold shimmered around her to make her outline unclear, especially when she moved. I couldn't tell if it was fabric or mist. The blur of her wings made the hazy glow I'd been seeing.

Immediately the tiny angel came to a stop, focusing on my voice. She blinked in surprise, her eyes glowing like the sun. "I lost your song, Madison," she said. "I couldn't hear your soul anymore. Stop what you're doing. I can't see you."

It worked! I thought ecstatically. If my guardian angel couldn't see me, then neither would a reaper or timekeeper. "I'm invisible," I said, gazing at her in wonder.

"I can see that," she snapped, weaving in agitation. "Now stop it. It has to be a mistake. I can barely hear your soul singing. I can't protect you if I can't see you."

I moved my arm, seeing that it had a shiny white edge to it now, kind of what a black wing looked like on the end. Curious, I tried to pick up my glass. I shivered as the cold of the pop went straight to my bones, and I couldn't seem to tighten my fingers enough to get a grip. I wondered why I could sit on a chair without passing through, until I moved the balled-up straw wrapper. It must be that I was substantial enough to have some effect on the world, but not a whole lot. Taking a walk in a windstorm would probably be a bad idea. Maybe that's how Barnabas could fly.

"Madison, are you still there?" Josh whispered.

"Yes," I said, allowing a few more lines to remain as the future became the present. The angel sighed in relief, and Josh's eyes shifted to mine.

"Damn!" he whispered. "I can sort of see you. Jeez, Madison. This is bizarre. Can I touch you?"

"I wouldn't," Grace said as she hovered over the table, but I shrugged, and he reached out to put his fingers on my wrist. We both shuddered at the eerie sensation of contact. His fingers seemed to burn, and I jerked away at the same time he did.

"Cold," he said, hiding his hand under the table.

"Can you hear me better?" I asked, and he nodded. This had to be the weirdest thing I'd ever done. Destroying the amulet's threads as they turned from future to present was almost easy now. Like humming to background music when you're doing your homework. I'd done it. I'd finally learned something, and the relief for that was almost enough to make me cry.

"Excellent," Josh said, smiling as I went totally invisible again, much to Grace's disgust. "If you can do this, you can take that amulet for sure."

I laughed, and Josh pressed into the cushions.

"Don't laugh when you've ghosted like that," he said as he looked around the coffee shop. "It's really weird. Man, I'm going to have more nightmares."

I think I flashed visible for an instant when the front door opened, surprising me. I tightened my awareness on the amulet's threads, taking out a chunk of them and going dizzy for an instant until I steadied myself and fell into a pattern of destroying them in a smooth progression. I looked up when

Josh stiffened, seeing two people angling toward us, a third still at the counter, ordering.

I froze, wondering what to do. They'd seen Josh here alone. I couldn't just pop back into existence. But then I made a face when I recognized the tall girl in a designer tank top and short shorts as Amy, looking like summer incarnate as she sauntered over with Len behind her. Parker was at the counter paying for everything as usual. All three were on the track team.

Amy hung with the popular girls. Nice on the surface, but I'd tried to be a popular girl at my old school long enough to know that surface was often just that. She usually went with Len unless she was punishing him for cheating on her. But after having seen Len in action, I didn't feel sorry for her at all.

Len was a big guy, and he liked to slam kids up against lockers when the teachers weren't looking, laughing and playing up to them like it was a joke so they would willingly trade the humiliation for five seconds of being noticed by the popular guy. Though he wasn't the fastest person on the track team, he was charming—especially in his own mind—and he treated girls like ice cream—sampling a new flavor each month for a day or two. He was good-looking enough that the girls he went after let him get away with it, a fact that irritated me to no end.

Parker seemed nice enough, but I had a feeling they let him hang with them because he put up with their abuse, hungry to belong. Seeing him paying for everything now made me ill. I'd almost been a Parker once, trying anything, enduring everything, even making excuses for others in my effort to belong. If not for Wendy, I might have caved and become that person. It wasn't worth it. Not by a long shot.

"Hi, Josh," Amy said cheerfully as she cocked her hip and put one hand flat on the table. "So where's Madison A-very-freaky-girl? Still pushing her bike down the road?"

Peeved, I scooted into the corner of the booth, cutting threads like mad to stay invisible.

Josh gave her a sour look as he did a hand-slapping thing with Len. "She's really nice, okay? Don't call her that anymore."

"Oh?" Amy sat, making me shrink back farther. "You're the one who started it."

I scrambled up and climbed over the seat to stand on the cushion of the adjacent booth when Len sat and Amy shifted down.

"That was before I got to know her," Josh said, his ears going red. "She's cool."

Amy scoffed, picking up my shopping bag with a pinkie and moving it closer so she could look inside. "Doing a little shopping?" she taunted, and if I could pick things up, I would have shoved a chunk of ice down the back of her shirt. "We saw you at the mall."

Josh's eyes scanned the room, looking for me, probably. If I was smart, I'd duck into the girls' bathroom, go visible, and come back. But I stayed. "It's Madison's. She's taking pictures tomorrow and needed a new card," he said, taking the bag back.

"You should give her a chance. You'd like her."

"Doubt it," Amy said dryly, then took the iced coffee that Parker had brought over. "Where does she live? Hidden Lake? Like there was ever a lake in that middle-class slum."

My teeth gritted, and I snipped a rush of lines before I became visible.

"That's really classy, Amy," Josh said bitingly. I glanced at Parker, knowing he lived down the street from me. His lips were pressed together and he wouldn't look at anyone.

Amy brought her knees up, sitting sideways with her feet on the bench seat to look coy. "I think Josh is sweet on his new little friend. God! She has purple hair. What a freak."

Josh exhaled slowly, eyes down. If I hadn't already been dead, I would have died right then. My fingers reached to touch my hair, and I vowed to put a green streak in it next week. Beside me, I could see Grace starting to get angry, her eyes almost shooting sparks.

"I told you that you look better without these," Amy said as she took Josh's glasses off and set them on the table. "She's weird and a bitch," she said, so casually it shocked me. "You said it yourself. Why are you hanging with such a Meg!"

It sounded innocuous, but I was up on my Brit slang. It meant Most Embarrassing Gal or Guy. Great.

Looking pained, Josh glanced up. "I said that before I knew her, okay?" he said loudly. "What is it to you, anyway? Still mad about me dumping you last year?"

Len laughed, reaching to give Parker a high five. "Right before the prom!" he said, cramming three fries in his mouth. "If I'd had a camera, I'd be a millionaire."

My eyes widened. Whoa. He dumped her, then took me out? No wonder she hated me.

Amy's eyes narrowed. "Oh, for God's sake. She's so freaked that even the Goths won't have her. A total case!"

Len leaned forward with his arms flat on the table. "Amy's right," he said seriously. "You can do better than her. You're a senior."

A total case? He could do better? My emotions swung full circle, and I gritted my teeth, so ticked I could scream. I should've walked away. I should have walked away and not listened.

Grace's beating wings gave off a tight hum, and I heard her say, "There once was a girl from Lake Powell, whose mouth was something quite foul. The crap she did spew, like an overfull loo, till I smacked her right into a wall."

Depressed, I sank down in the seat of the next booth over, still cutting threads, still invisible. "That doesn't rhyme," I whispered, wiping under my eye. Damn it, I wasn't going to cry because of what *Amy* said.

"Maybe not," Grace said tartly, "but that's what's going to happen."

"Shake her off, dude," Len said. "Do it, or she's going to be hanging on you all year."

"You ever think I might want to hang with her all year?" Josh said angrily. "She's a lot more fun than you, so afraid of what everyone else thinks you can't even pick out your own clothes without calling someone. And that's her drink, weenis."

"I can't believe you brought her here!" Amy said loudly. "This is our place!"

I perked up, starting to feel better when Josh said, "Better go, unless you want to see her. You might have to be nice, and a smile would probably crack your perfect face, Amy."

Quietly I got up to look over the back of the booth seat. Josh was red with anger. Len seemed unsure, and Parker was clearly uncomfortable as he messed with his iced coffee. In a quick motion, Amy shoved her feet into Len to make him move so she could get out. "Later, dude," Len said as he and Amy stalked off.

Parker gave Josh an uneasy look and stood. From the front of the hangout/skate park, Amy mocked, "Bye, Josh," as she waited by the door.

I knew my expression was ugly as Parker followed Len to the door. Josh exhaled, then whispered, "Madison, I'm sorry. Are you still here? They're jerks. Don't listen to them. I said that stuff before I knew you. I'm an ass. Please come back. I'm sorry. I . . . I like your hair."

Frustrated, I scrambled over the back of the booth seat and slid down. The seat was still warm from Amy. *Yuck.* I focused on my amulet, taking a moment to let the lines form, violet threads from the stone, to me, and to the present, grounding me in a brand-new past. Josh's gaze darted to mine when I became visible, but I couldn't look at him. The guardian angel seemed to relax, going to sit in the light fixture, where her faint glow was lost. "Nothing like knowing your spot in the pecking order, huh?" I muttered.

Josh shifted uneasily. "They're idiots," he said as he pushed my drink back to me. "I'm really sorry. I shouldn't have said those things before. I didn't know you then."

I fiddled with the straw, unable to meet his eyes. "They are your friends."

He shrugged. "Not really. Amy thinks her sweat doesn't stink. Len is a bully I wouldn't let pound me in third grade— we have a weird truce in which we pretend to be friends so he doesn't have to try to beat me up again. Parker . . . I think they let him hang around because they need someone to pick on, and he's so desperate to belong that he lets them."

I took a sip of my drink, shivering as the icy soda slid down. If this was who Josh hung with, no surprise he liked me. I was starting to feel better, though, especially when I heard a muffled yelp from the parking lot and saw Amy step back from Len's truck, her hand over her face. She was yelling something about her nose. Beside me, a haze of light giggled.

"Thanks," I said shyly to Josh. "For sticking up for me, I mean."

Josh's smile made my heart flip-flop. "Forget it," he said as he picked at his fries.

But I wouldn't. Ever.

His blue eyes met mine as he put his glasses back on. "And you can go invisible."

"Ye-e-e-ep," I drawled, suffused with a feeling of satisfaction. Leaning back, I laced my fingers and extended my arms, cracking my knuckles. It was hard to stay upset with jerks when you could go invisible. "Kairos doesn't have a chance. All we have to do is find a quiet spot, you distance yourself enough from me that black wings can sense you, Kairos shows up, and I slip in invisible-like and lift his amulet." I smiled. "Then we run away fast, and he'll have to leave until he can make a new amulet."

He laughed at the running-away part, and I felt good. Finishing his fries, he glanced at his watch. It had more buttons than a calculator. "So, we doing this?"

I glanced out the windows at the lengthening shadows. "Yup. Not here, though. Do you know of an alley or something?"

"Mmmm, how about Rosewood Park?"

Grace's hum grew louder, and she dropped down from the light fixture to hover inches before my face. "Madison, I'm just a first-sphere angel and all, but don't do this. Don't go invisible again. Wait for Barnabas. Please. It feels dangerous."

Waving her away, I said, "I can't wait for Barnabas. Besides, if you can't see me, neither can Kairos. You can't catch what you can't see."

"What about other things, Madison?" she asked, worried.

"There *are* other things. If I can't see you, maybe something else can."

That was a nasty thought, and I sat back against the hard seat, pondering it.

"What did she say?" Josh asked, trying to see her by following my eyes.

I sighed dramatically to downplay her concern. "She doesn't want me to go invisible because she can't see me. Thinks it's dangerous."

An indignant harrumph filled my ear. "It's not that I can't see you. It's that something else might be able to."

Josh's eyebrows went higher. "I didn't know it wasn't safe."

"It's safe enough," I protested. "Besides, if we don't face Kairos now, what happens tonight? It's not like you can spend the night at my house. My dad's cool, but telling him we need to stay together so my guardian angel can keep you safe isn't going to work. Personally, I'd rather face Kairos now than my dad after I break curfew."

Josh made a face. "I don't especially want to get in trouble, either."

Frustrated, I took a sip of pop. I'd be grounded for a month if I didn't show up for dinner—if I was lucky. But Josh wouldn't make it through the night if we didn't do something. "Breaking curfew one too many times was how I got shipped up here," I said softly, almost to myself. "Besides, what will that get us? Come morning, when they track us down, you'll be yanked to the other side of town and I'll be locked in my room. Fat lot of good that will do us. No, we face Kairos now, while we have some choice of how and when."

"Madison, no," Grace protested, her wings going so fast I think Josh could almost see her glow. "Wait until Ron or Barnabas gets back. Do it then."

An exasperated noise slipped from me. "If either one of them were here, I wouldn't have to do it at all. That's the whole point!"

"But I don't think you're doing it right," she said, backing up slightly. "I should be able to hear your soul singing even when you go invisible, and I can't! Please don't do this."

"Either we do this thing now," I said, hoping Josh was getting the gist of this, "or we break curfew, buying us only the time between now and when our parents catch us. I'm not willing to risk Josh's life in the hope that Ron will be back by then. So unless you want to stay with Josh tonight, we have no reason to wait for Barnabas."

I froze and Josh looked up at me, wonder in his eyes.

"Hey, that's not a bad idea," I said, pulling forward in the seat as Grace hovered backward. "My guardian angel could go with you tonight. You'd be safe and neither of us will get in trouble."

"Huh?" It was a tiny utterance, sounding odd coming from a ball of light. "No. I've been charged to watch you. Ron himself set me the task to keep you out of trouble. Safe."

"Yeah, well, if you don't go with Josh, then I'm going to find Kairos and get into major trouble."

Josh leaned in conspiratorially. "What is she saying?"

Smiling, I tapped my fingernails on the table. The answer had been staring me in the face all afternoon, singing limericks. "If my guardian angel stays with you, you'll be okay. She can hide your aura, same as me."

"What about you?" Josh asked as Grace swung back and forth in agitation.

"I'll be fine!" I said confidently. "He doesn't know my new amulet resonance. Doesn't know where I live. They can't find me unless they find you first. And if they do, I'll just go invisible." I turned to the ball of light. "So you see, it's in my best interest that you go with Josh."

"No," she said forcefully. "It doesn't work that way. I was told to stay with you."

"And I'm telling you to stay with him!" I exclaimed, then lowered my voice as three skinny guys came out of the snake pit with their boards tucked under their arms.

The glowing ball of light came so close to my face I jerked back. "Look, missy," Grace said sharply, "you can't tell me to go anywhere. I have my order from Ron, and, baby, you're not Ron."

Frustrated, I leaned forward until she backed up. "Go with him, Grace," I intoned. "Now. Until I say different. Otherwise, I'm going ghost and doing this tonight."

"Grace?" the guardian angel whispered as her glow dimmed. "You gave me a name?"

Josh was starting to look uncomfortable, which I could understand, since he couldn't see her and it looked like I was yelling at him. Lips pressed, I glared at the glow over the table. I refrained from pointing a finger at the stubborn angel, but just. "Grace—"

"I'll go with him," she said, her glow briefly becoming brighter. It was meek and mild, and she shocked my next words right out of me. "Madison," she continued, "if you get me into trouble, I'm going to be so mad at you! I've never been a guardian before. You're my first charge, and if I mess this up, I have to go back to sensitivity training for the living."

I stared as Grace shifted a bare three inches to move closer to Josh.

"I'll stay with him," she said, her voice flowing like liquid.

Josh was watching my stunned surprise with an inquiring look. "What just happened?"

Puzzled, I straightened. "Uh, she's going to stay with you," I said, and he exhaled in relief.

Eyebrows high, he leaned back. "So . . . we're going to wait?"

I nodded, much to Grace's relief. "But not any longer than tomorrow," I added, and she bristled, if the orange sparks she was shooting out meant anything. "If Barnabas or Ron doesn't show by morning, then I'm going to call Kairos out. Take his amulet."

"Shoot 'em down. Do your stuff," Josh added, laughing. "Good. That will give us some time to come up with a plan better than 'get him.' Tell you what. I'll come over tomorrow morning to pick you up to go to the carnival, and we'll go out to Rosewood Park instead to take care of Kairos. That way, you can get your angel back right away."

"*That* sounds like a plan," I said, glancing at Grace as she made an odd noise: part disapproval, part evil planning, part frustration. I didn't like the deception, but what would I tell my dad? *Hi, Dad. Evil Father Time is going to kill Josh. Not to worry, since I'm going to steal his source of power again. I'll be back before lunch. Kiss-kiss!*

"I'll get you home then," Josh said, standing up and gathering his stuff. "Do you have my cell number?"

"No," I said, distracted as I thought over what just happened. Dang, I had given an angel an order, and she had taken it. Went from outright defiance to agreement. And as I drank the last of my pop so we could get out of there, I shivered.

Me commanding angels. That couldn't be good.

Seven

The sky was blue, the temperature was fabulous, and there was just a hint of a breeze. It was a perfect day. Or it would be, if I could get back inside before my dad woke up.

A few streets over, the morning traffic was a soft hush, and I quietly leaned my bike against the side of the garage and squinted at my watch in the post-dawn light. Six forty. Dad liked to sleep in on Saturday, but seeing as I had to be out the door in less than an hour, it was likely that he'd be up by now. I should have come home sooner, but it had been hard to trust Grace and leave Josh's street—especially after spotting that black wing on the distant horizon.

Josh and I had agreed to text each other all night, and when his messages had stopped around two, I'd snuck out to make sure he was okay. He'd been sleeping, but now I was stiff, dew-wet, and in danger of being grounded anyway.

I usually spent my dark hours, when everyone was sleeping, either on the Internet or on the roof with Barnabas, hammering my head against a wall, but the skills I'd developed sneaking out of my mom's house were never left to go fallow for long. At least once a week I would escape to wander around in the dark, pretending I could evade Barnabas and boredom both.

So when Josh's text messages had stopped, it had been a no-brainer to sneak out. There had been no black wings circling his house, but leaving hadn't sat well with me. I'd spent the rest of the night behind a tree talking to Grace, trying not to feel like a stalker. I didn't like sneaking out or lying to my dad, but it wasn't as if I had much of a choice.

The neighbor's dog barked at me, and I reached up behind the light fixture for the treat I'd put there last week, buying the golden retriever's silence. Seeing the dog tail-wagging happy, I carefully stepped up onto the silver trash can—the one I religiously replaced exactly where I wanted it after trash pickup. Gripping the outside of the garage's windowsill with one hand, I reached for the low roof with the other, swinging my foot up for purchase on the top of the window before throwing my other leg over to land stomach-down on the shingles. Pleased, I sat up, brushing the grit off as the dog panted at me, begging for more.

"Still got it," I whispered, smiling. It had been a stunt like this that had gotten me shipped up here to my dad's house. It was that, my mom had said, or she was going to put bars on my windows.

Hunched, I crab-walked to the peak of the garage roof, ignoring the lone black wing drifting aimlessly on the horizon. Easing down to my stomach, I peered over the top to find Mrs. Walsh sitting at her little kitchen table with curlers in her hair, reading the paper. "There you are, you old bat," I whispered.

I swear, the woman waited for me, itching to catch me at something. She reminded me of the bored, middle-aged women my mom made me be nice to over lunch in her attempts to raise money for whatever cause she was championing at the time. I kind of missed the formal teas, though, and the inevitable pre-tea battle over my newest hair color or temporary tattoo carefully placed to be seen while I was in my prissy-girl clothes. Seeing my mom dressed up in her perfumed best and being charming when I knew she wanted to throttle the tightfisted women for being so shortsighted had been a lot of fun. Maybe I was more like my mom than I thought.

A smile quirked the corners of my lips as I lay on the roof, thinking of my mom. I had talked to her last night when she had called to check on me, her trouble-radar working even from Florida. I honestly didn't know how she did it.

Twisting onto my side, I wedged my fingers into my pocket and pulled out my phone. A little jolt of excitement went through me when I saw Josh's text. He was up—which I knew already, having heard his alarm go off—and he would be here in half an hour. I shot off a C U, then punched speed-dial three. Seconds later, I heard a faint ring and Mrs. Walsh stood, vanishing deeper into the house. I couldn't help my grin.

The instant her back was turned, I closed the phone. Humming the music to *Mission Impossible*, I got to my feet and slid down the other side of the roof, easily making the hop to the roof over my room. Impatient, I wedged my screen back off the window and eased it to the carpet. Sitting on the sill, I took off my shoes and slipped inside. I couldn't leave wet marks on the floor to give me away. I'd learned that the hard way after a midnight walk on the beach in Florida and my sandy rug turned into a week's grounding.

My smile faded at the familiar sounds of my dad's shower and the smell of coffee.

"Great," I whispered, not knowing if my dad had looked in to make sure I'd gotten up before he hit the shower. I knew from experience that pillows under the comforter didn't work, so I'd left my bed unmade, hoping he'd think I was in my bathroom. Worried, I replaced the screen with fumbling fingers. I should have trusted Grace, and left sooner.

With nervous haste, I tugged my comforter up and tossed the pillows I'd shoved to the floor last night back on the bed. I hated getting home late. I was getting sloppy. I think my dad would have called me if he'd caught me sneaking out, but maybe not, wanting to see how much I'd dig myself into a lie before making me come clean. Though he was more easygoing than my mom, he had a devious streak in him. It was where I'd gotten it, I suppose.

My mom's picture on the mirror was smirking at me, and I turned it backward. Moving quickly, I stripped off yesterday's clothes and jumped into my shower to get rid of the night's chill. I had to get Kairos's new amulet today. I didn't have time to wait for Ron or Barnabas to rescue me. It was only a matter of time before Kairos tracked Josh or me down by process of elimination, and I couldn't take another night like the one I'd just gone through. I honestly didn't know how Barnabas or Grace did it.

Refreshed by the quick splash-and-dash, I toweled off and threw on some clothes, picking a set of yellow tights to hide the slowly fading rug burn from the boat, a short purple skirt, and a matching top over a black tank top. My sneakers were still wet, but after drying off the bottoms, I put them on, wincing at the damp and wondering if my dad would notice. It wasn't like I could wear something else. They were made for this outfit. And if Amy didn't like it, she could choke on my individuality. This was who I was, and I was tired of trying to fit in. Besides, Josh liked my purple hair.

Smug, I leaned across the bed and dragged my camera over. I still had five minutes or so before Josh got here. Time enough to send a picture to Wendy. She'd e-mailed me last night with a shot of her and my old boyfriend, taken on the beach at sunset. They looked good together, and after I got over my mad,

I realized it was time to let go. I'd been trying to hold on to the way it had been, but I couldn't. It was already gone. I was e-mailing the past, trying to make it my future, when my future was somewhere else. But that didn't mean I couldn't drive her mad with envy with my yellow tights.

Standing, I tugged the wrinkles out of my skirt, hoping the day was going to be as warm as the skies predicted. Holding the camera in front of me, I found a martial arts pose, then shifted my hand until I was in the viewfinder, reflected in the mirror above my dresser. Annoyed, I set the camera down. My bed would be in the picture, and it was still a carefully contrived mess.

Tidying it was easy, and I put the vampire teddy bear Wendy had given me in the place of honor between the lacy pillows my dad had thought I'd like. The room was nothing like the dark cave at my mom's house. The white dresser decorated with rosebuds didn't do it for me. Neither did the antique-looking comforter or the slew of lacy pillows that I threw off the bed every night to convince my dad that I was sleeping. The pale rose color of the walls was comforting, though, going well with the cream carpet. It was painfully obvious that my dad had forgotten I wasn't six anymore and had filled the room with frilly pink-and-white girl stuff I'd shunned for years.

My fingers that were arranging the pillows slowed as I realized my room was almost identical to my room before we had left. Sort of like the kitchen and the living room, all carrying whispers of my mother. He wasn't letting go, either.

My mood going introspective, I picked up the camera. It had hurt not seeing Wendy every day. We'd known each other since fifth grade, and she was probably the reason I'd never made it completely into the popular crowd, now that I thought about it. She was more oddball than me, but I'd refused to ditch her when I'd finally been invited in, trying to bring her along with me instead. Wendy had quietly stood by me with her environmentally conscious lunch tote and her political music blaring, knowing I was making a mistake but confident enough in herself to wait for me to realize it. Expecting to find another friend like her amid the Amys and Lens looked really slim. Josh, though, was turning out to be cool.

The shutter clicked, and I dropped my arm and my smile both. I plugged the camera into my laptop. At least that had come with me from my mom's and it was suitably dark and broody. The background was of my favorite alternative band. Wendy had introduced me to them, but to be honest, I liked the aggressive noise more than the message behind it.

Immediately the picture uploaded, and I opened it to check out the resolution.

My skin still retained its beach tan, which was weird, but I chalked it up to my not having a real body. The purple tips of my hair were starting to fade, though. It hadn't grown at all since I died, and I wondered if I was going to look like this forever. My eyes went to my small chest, and I sighed. Not good. So not good. But then I looked closer at the picture, frowning.

"Oh, crap," I whispered, alarm icing through me. I could see my bed behind me. I mean, I could see *through* me to my bed. Scared, I looked at my hands. They looked solid to me, but the picture said different.

"Oh, crap . . ." I stood in front of the mirror, fear making the memory of my heart pound. I looked okay there, too, but when I picked up my camera and looked at myself through the lens . . .

"Oh, crap!" I said a third time. It wasn't obvious, but there was a hint of shadow where the bed was, and even a shape of pillows.

This was so not what I needed. Josh was ready to knock on my door to carry me off to battle the evil reaper master and steal his amulet. I didn't have time to be substance challenged. Worried, I gripped my amulet and loosened my focus, trying to jump into that misty state I'd been in yesterday to check things out. Maybe I'd broken too many threads when I'd practiced going invisible? Maybe I'd begun an unraveling that I couldn't fix? Grace had told me not to do it. But I'd never know if I didn't stop shaking!

My time spent with Barnabas on my roof learning to relax paid off, and slowly my pulse vanished. My teeth unclenched, and I found in my thoughts the hazy imagination of my life thread and the lacy spider-silk net joining it to the cosmos.

Immediately the knot in my gut relaxed. The threads of connection were obvious, tying me to the present as the future slipped into the now. My thoughts were throwing out new threads as fast as the sun ticked across the sky, pulling me along with the rest of the world. I hadn't broken anything.

"Then why can I see through myself?" I whispered. Panic subsiding to concern, I pulled up my picture of my shoes on my laptop. I'd been in them at the time I'd taken the photo. Squinting, I looked again, but the little I could see of my ankles seemed normal. Relieved, I dumped both pictures into the trash and emptied it. Wendy would have to do without. No way was I ever going to let anyone take another picture of me.

The sound of a vehicle coming up the quiet residential street made me lean out the window. A smile grew when I saw Josh's old blue pickup. He was here. Finally.

Scrambling, I unplugged my camera, grabbed my wallet, slapped my back pocket to make sure I had my phone, and started into the hall. *Please, please, please don't let my dad know I've been out this morning.* This could all come to a nasty, screeching halt really fast.

"Madison?" my dad's voice echoed faintly. "Josh is here!"

He sounded unbothered, and I exhaled. "Be right there!" I called as I flounced down the stairs in relief. My dad waited at the bottom beside the front door, looking casual in jeans and a lightweight shirt, smiling. I'd done it again, but just.

"Don't forget the printer," he said, handing me a small

camera case. "I put extra paper and ink in there," he said as I looped the strap over my shoulder, feeling guilty. "Enough to take as many pictures as you want."

"Jeez, Dad," I said as I looked inside. "How many pictures do you think people are going to want?" I wasn't even going to be there. How was I going to explain not using any of this? But I had to confront Kairos now, disapproving Grace or not. If she really thought I was in danger, then she ought to go get Ron.

"I know you," my dad said. "When you get behind a camera, you can't help yourself. Consider it my contribution. It's tax deductible!" he said, his smile turning into a wide grin that made his long face seem to light up. "And I like your pictures," he said, giving me a hug good-bye. "Everyone else will too. You look nice today. You were right. Purple is your color." His expression went thoughtful, and he looked out at Josh's truck. "You and Barnabas aren't having trouble, are you?"

I jerked to a stop. *Oh, yeah.* "Dad, I told you Barnabas and I are just friends."

"He hangs around an awful lot for being just a friend," my dad warned.

"Just a friend," I said firmly. "And he knows it. I'm only spending the day with Josh. It's not a big deal. If we're lucky, Barnabas will show up, and we can do the fair together."

Nodding, he put a hand on my shoulder. "Sounds like you've got it under control," he said, and I strangled what would have been a hysterical-sounding laugh. "Have fun today."

"I will," I said, my worry and guilt rising. I could almost hear Grace singing about the girl who was a liar and fell into a fryer. "Thanks for the printer and everything." I was such a bad daughter. But he'd known what he was getting when my mom shipped me up here—mostly.

My dad followed me as far as the porch when Josh got out of his truck. "Hi, Mr. A.," Josh said, waving. He was wearing jeans and a T-shirt, but I could see his gym bag shoved up against the back, window dressing for today's performance, I guess.

Scanning for black wings, I hurriedly got in his truck and slammed the door, anxious to leave. The Harley bell was glowing, and I leaned forward as I put my seat belt on. "Grace, do I look okay to you?" I asked, remembering my picture. "Am I thin? I mean, transparent?"

The thrum of her wings grew obvious. "No," she said, hovering before me. "Why?"

I took a breath to tell her, then changed my mind when Josh opened his door. "Later."

Josh slid back in behind the wheel and looked askance at me as he shut his door. "Feeling guilty?" he teased, seeing my worry.

Rolling my eyes, I grimaced. "Josh," I said, trying to find a worldly air, "the stuff I've done when my mother thought I was sleeping would curl your hair." He laughed and I added, "The first time I ran into Kairos, I died. I'm a little nervous, okay?"

I wasn't going to tell him I'd camped out beside his house last night after he fell asleep. The guy did have his pride.

Josh looked over his shoulder and backed up into the street. "Sorry," he said softly.

He slowly accelerated toward town, and I waved bye to my dad standing on the porch. For crying out loud, could he be any more embarrassing? "Hey, thanks for texting this morning," I said. "I saw a black wing around dawn. How about you?"

"Nothing." Frowning, he shoved his glasses up and made the turn to go to Rosewood Park. "I'm glad we had some breathing space, but we've got to get Kairos's amulet this morning. I can't take much more of Grace."

"Really?" I questioned, and the angel made a huff of sound.

"I ran out of hot water in my shower last night, and I'm sure it was her," he said. "The Internet wouldn't work, either. And my brother kept stubbing his toe all freaking night. Madison, she's driving me nuts."

From the Harley bell came a tinkling laughter. "Josh was going to cut his face with his razor if he tried to use it without a mirror, and his brother was going to do something naughty, so I broke the signal to the Internet. And every time he swore, I made him stub his toe."

I looked at the golden haze about the gently swaying bell. *Josh had shaved?* My lips pressed together as I remembered that stoplight crashing down. Clearly Grace didn't mind causing chaos if it was less horrific than the trouble she imagined she was preventing. "Nothing happened last night, Grace," I said to soothe her. "By noon, everything will be fine." I thought of that picture and the black wings, and I took a deep breath I didn't need. "Josh is okay, and he wouldn't be if you hadn't stayed with him. Don't you feel good about that?"

"Ye-e-e-e-s," she drawled, sounding too pleased with herself for my peace of mind. I looked across the truck to Josh as we bounced along. "She's awfully smug," I said in warning.

"Great," he said. "Grace," he said, clearly more comfortable today talking to the air than he was when I left him last night. "It doesn't matter if we get a flat tire on the way to the park, we're still going to do this, only we'll do it in the road instead of a nice quiet patch of ground where no one else will get hurt if things go wrong."

The bell swayed gently. "Nothing is wrong," she almost purred.

"I don't like this," I muttered. It was a feeling that grew the closer we got to the park and the more cars I saw. Some were even pulled onto the side of the road. Couples with kids were getting out, nervous from the traffic. Rosewood wasn't that big a park. There was never a lot of activity there, even on a Saturday.

"Uh, Madison?" Josh questioned as he pulled into the park and found himself in a line. A van tucked in behind him, and we were trapped. Josh inched forward to a woman wearing a school cap. She was obviously directing traffic, and everyone was stopping to talk to her.

Grace started to laugh, and I realized what had happened. The event had been moved from Blue Diamond Park to here. Great. Just great. No wonder Grace was giggling.

"Grace!" I yelled, and Josh shot me a look to be quiet as he rolled his window down. I didn't have time for this! I had to face Kairos and get my life back!

The woman with the hat peered at us in the sun. "Participant or attendee?" she asked.

From the bell came a chiming, "A girl named Madison Avery, deemed she was smart and savory. So an order she gave, to an angel made slave, but soon she was shaken and wavery."

Josh leaned out the window. "Uh, participant. I'm running the track and she's taking pictures."

I held up my camera in explanation, but my conscience was smarting. I hadn't come here to take pictures, but here I was.

The woman squinted at the full parking lot. "Drive right through to the end. We've got participants parking on the grass. Just follow the yellow balloons."

"Follow the yellow balloons!" Grace chimed, whizzing around the cab, delighted at her success at keeping us from confronting Kairos.

Josh nodded, but he didn't move forward. "Why aren't we at Blue Diamond?"

The woman's eyebrows went up. "Oh, it was the oddest thing!" she exclaimed. "The sprinklers came on and ran all night. It's mud to your ankles, so everything was moved out here. Thanks for helping today. Be sure to stop at the hospitality tent."

There was no way we were getting out of here anytime soon, and I leaned forward. "Do you know who I can talk to about setting up a table to develop my pictures?" I asked.

Adjusting her hat, the woman thought. "I'd try Ms. Cartwright," she said, looking over the cars to the park. "She's overseeing everything. She'll be at the green tent."

My head bobbed. I'd seen Ms. Cartwright in the halls at school, but I didn't know what she taught. "Thank you," I said, and I settled back in my seat, jittery. *Damn it, Grace.*

Josh crept forward. "Follow the yellow balloons," he said sourly.

Grace zipped from one end of the cab to the other. "Follow the yellow balloons!"

I sighed, and my camera felt heavy on my chest. "Grace, you're evil," I whispered.

"This stuff is easy," she said smugly. Apparently I'd been forgiven, since she sat on my shoulder and made my ears ring with the vibration from her wings.

Josh eyed the parked cars as we passed, and sighed. "We can't fight Kairos here."

Grace giggled, and I made a face. "Nope," I said. "I don't think we can leave, either."

From my shoulder, Grace said, "If you try, you're going to

get a flat tire, Joshua."

Joshua, I thought, curious. "Don't try to leave," I said as we neared the exit. "You'll get a flat. Miss Limerick here doesn't want us getting into any trouble." *Puppy presents, maybe we could walk out of here. Grace wouldn't make one of us break a leg or something, would she?*

"Limerick?" Josh asked, and I shook my head.

"You really don't want to know." *Yeah, Grace would probably break something, laughing all the way.*

He was concentrating on the parking lot, and I gripped the door handle when we went onto the grass and lurched in the ruts, following the cant-wise line of cars to the end until we parked in the shade of a spreading oak. The sound of our doors shutting seemed to echo as a handful of other people parked and got out of their vehicles. Josh had his gym bag with him, and my camera bag was over my shoulder. The air was crisp and cool under the tree, and I could sense the excitement as people slowly migrated from their cars to the open field. It had been a long, miserable night watching Josh's house, but the fact that I was sort of see-through had me worried about going invisible again so soon. I could put Kairos off for a few hours. Take a few pictures. Not be so much of a liar.

"Grace, you stay with Josh. Please," I added belatedly as the glowing ball of light that was her wings took on a harsh hue. "He can't do his event with me running beside him."

Her wings darkened to almost nothing, and a subdued

"okay" came out of her.

I didn't trust her show of meekness, and we slowly wove through the parked cars to the field. Halfway there I brought my camera up and snapped a picture of a child, awe on his face as he touched a clown's nose. A smile came over me as I looked at it in the viewer. The sky was a brilliant blue, and the clown's makeup was stark and perfect. Bright and bold.

"Good day for a run," Josh said slowly.

I nodded, feeling the air in my lungs. "I suppose we can do this awhile," I said, not wanting a meteor to drop on me if I tried to leave.

"I pledged to run a couple of laps," he said. "I can't collect the money otherwise."

Seeing his desire to run, I shifted my bag higher up my shoulder. It was heavy with my promise. Kairos could wait a couple of hours as long as Grace was watching Josh. "So, see you about noon?" I said as I made motions to head off to the green tent.

Josh smiled, the sun in his hair. "Watch out for Amy."

I smirked. It took skill to take a good picture. It took more to take a bad one. "You bet."

He nodded and turned. I waited a moment to be sure Grace went with him, then headed for the green tent and Ms. Cartwright.

Eight

The wind shifted the purple tips of my hair in front of the camera, and I waited until it cleared. I slowly followed Josh's loping body around the track, zooming in as he rounded the turn and I could see his face. He breathed in, and I snapped the shot, immediately moving the camera from my eye to see what I'd captured in the viewing screen.

I couldn't help my smile. He looked suitably tortured, eyes pinched and mouth open. Sweat made his hair stick to his forehead. Behind him were the blurry and colorful shapes of the other runners. In the foreground was a hazy ball of light anyone else would say was a camera artifact, but I knew it was Grace. Josh would be glad to see some evidence of her.

The sound of running feet pulled my attention up. "Looking good, Josh!" I shouted, and I got a quick wave in return. He wasn't as tired as the picture indicated. And it wasn't a race. The track team was simply making sure someone was on the field at all times, sort of a daylong marathon. At the outside of the track was a much slower-moving group of nonathletes. It was as much a social event as anything else, and I could hear the ladies talking about their kids as they power walked, earning dollars per lap to help buy a new activity bus.

I raised my camera and got a shot when one of the women laughed, catching her in a moment of happiness. Their participant badges were clearly visible, and I toyed with the idea of showing it to Ms. Cartwright to see if she wanted to use it in next year's promotion.

Turning, I spotted Covington High's girls' track team stretching under the shade of the birch trees. Colorful gym bags littered the grass, and I took a few shots, making sure Amy was not looking her best. Zooming in, I focused on the bandage over her purple nose, bruised and swollen, thanks to Grace, and with a grin, I took a really bad one with her mouth hanging open.

"Never tick off the photographer," I whispered, feeling good about catching her in more than one awkward, unflattering pose.

I'd been taking pictures now for about three hours and I was starting to get tired, even as my long-fallow photography muscles enjoyed the workout. The camera card I'd bought yesterday had been a godsend. I'd already filled it up once, taking time to dump everything into the printer before clearing it out and going back in search of more timely moments.

"Like that one," I whispered when I saw a man holding his child close and high to his face. He was pointing to one of the walkers on the field, and the baby, a girl by the looks of the bow and frills, was following his gaze. The man's face glowed as he talked to his daughter. Behind them was a stroller with a huge diaper bag shoved under it and a handful of toys tied to the front bar.

I took a picture of the stroller just because I thought it was cool that something so small needed so much stuff, then focused on the man and his child, waiting until the little girl recognized to whom he was pointing and made a delighted, wiggling gurgle. I snapped it, and the man turned as the camera whined.

I smiled, checking to make sure the ID tag Ms. Cartwright had given me was showing. "I'm taking photos to support the school," I said for the umpteenth time today. "Would you like me to print this for you? I can have it ready in about an hour."

His suspicion evaporated, turning into delight when I extended the back of the camera for him to see. "I didn't even know you were there," he said, jiggling the girl. "That is beautiful. How much?" He shifted his child to reach into his back pocket, and I waved my hand no.

"We're asking for a dollar, but you pay when you see them," I explained. "I've got them up at the green tent." The thump of fast feet came and went behind me, and the little girl squirmed, looking over my shoulder to follow the runners with her eyes.

"I'll be there," the man said as he scrambled to hold her. He gazed at the happy infant, saying in a falsetto, "Mommy will *love* to have a picture of us." His love for his daughter was still in his eyes when he turned back to me. "Thank you. I always forget to bring my camera to these things. Diapers, bottles, toys, and her snuggy, but never a camera."

Nodding, I gave him a reminder ticket before I waved at the cooing girl and walked away. It felt good to be out doing something instead of moping about in my room like it was a prison, missing my old friends. Yesterday at the Low D with Josh had been nice, even with Amy butting in and the looming trouble with Kairos. I'd forgotten how good it felt to be with someone and not afraid to be who I really was. Today, the sun was warm, the air was cool, and I was busy spending my dad's money on ink and paper. It didn't get much better than that.

From the nearby trees, I heard Amy shout an attention-getting, "Hi-i-i-i, Josh!" and I glanced up to see him run by again. Parker was out there with him now, and it looked like they were talking. I went to take a picture of them, but a CARD FULL message popped up.

"Cripes," I said with a sigh, then headed to the tent where I'd set up my table. Ms. Cartwright was really nice, not blinking an eye at my purple hair tips and skull earrings when she had given me a table where I could tape up some of the miscellaneous pictures that no one would likely claim.

"Madison! Is my picture done yet?" a tired, matronly voice called out, and my gaze went to a fatigued woman with three dusty boys. She looked ready to call it a day. I had a beautiful photo waiting of her and her boys on the merry-go-round before they'd worn her out and gotten cotton candy on their clothes. The sun glinting on the gold paint had matched their hair, and the straight up-and-down lines contrasted beautifully with the curling manes and bright paint on the horses. Side by side, the family resemblance that had changed little from age to age was striking. I'd printed out a second one for me just because I liked it.

"It's ready," I said, gesturing to the tent, but she was busy holding the two youngest apart as they argued about the goldfish they had won.

"I'll be along," she said quickly, then raised her voice to tell them they were going to kill the fish if they kept jiggling it like that.

No one even noticed me as I slipped inside the tent and wove my way to the back table. The shade was a welcome relief, and I eased in behind the long table to settle into my chair. A pleased sound escaped me when I realized a good portion of the photos were gone, even the ones that I'd thought no one would want. Happy, I plugged the camera into the printer and told it to print everything. It felt good to have my efforts appreciated.

The photos began coming out one by one, and I busied

myself arranging them on the table so people could find them. A shadow fell over me, and I looked up when Ms. Cartwright said admiringly, "Oh, I'll take that one." She reached for the picture falling into the hopper, adding, "Howard's my brother. I'd love to give that to him for his birthday. It's wonderful."

I glanced at a picture of a man sitting in the dunk tank, casually talking to someone in the crowd. He was dripping wet, and a blur of a ball was headed right for the target. What would happen next was obvious. "Really?" I asked, gratified. "Thanks," I added, handing it over.

She smiled at it briefly, her tired green eyes traveling fondly over the photo. "No, thank *you*. He's hard to buy for," she said as she tucked a long strand of hair that had escaped her thick ponytail behind an ear. "And this is a nice one of Mark," she said as the photo of the man and the little girl at the track came out. "He owns the car wash. He doesn't get a chance to be with Jem much. That's what they call their daughter. Jem." Her expression brightened and her fingers traveled over the pictures. "And Mrs. Hall. Oh my, look at that shoe size. No wonder she didn't pick her photo up. That hoof is front and center."

I fidgeted, embarrassed, but it was cool hearing about the people I'd been stealing bits of life from. It made me feel like I belonged somehow. I couldn't help but wonder if that was what I had been trying to do today—capture life because mine had basically stopped and the world hadn't. Continuing on without me. Circling like the seasons.

Looking closer, I squinted, wanting to take the picture out into the sun. It was almost as if I could see a shimmer about her. Her aura? *Nahhh.* "I thought the way the purple of the balloons went with the soles of her shoes was neat," I said, trying to explain why Mrs. Hall's back was so fascinating. *Neat? I think it's neat? God! I am such a nerd.*

"It is." Ms. Cartwright smiled at the photo of someone's van, the back doors open to show it was crammed to the top with undelivered papers. "You have a real knack for composition. Seeing what matters. What we miss if we don't slow down."

Another picture rolled out of the printer, and I set it on the table. "Thanks. I belonged to the photography club in my last school. I guess I picked up more than I thought."

Ms. Cartwright made an interested sound. "You're not on my class list. Why not? You have an eye for this."

She's the photography teacher? "Uh, I don't know," I said, suddenly nervous.

The woman's eyebrows arched, and she set the picture of Mrs. Hall down. "Oh-h-h-h, you're one of those, are you?" she said, and I stared blankly. "You don't want to be labeled a geek, so you color your hair purple and avoid anything that says you're smart."

"No," I said quickly, but she made a knowing face at me, and I rolled my gaze to the dusty ceiling. "Photography class is almost as bad as the chess club," I protested, and she laughed, taking up the next photo as it came out. I had a feeling the photography club hadn't helped in my quest for popularity at my old school. I didn't think it would help me much here, either. But why was I even trying for the popular crowd anymore?

"Reconsider it, Madison," she said as she scrutinized a photo. "There's a lot of talent here. I've been looking at what you've been doing, and you're capturing life in a way that is uniquely beautiful; even the ugliness is beautiful. That kind of an eye is hard to develop, if you'll pardon the pun. You might be able to get a scholarship if you applied yourself."

I was dead, yeah, but I'd probably still have to go to school and get a good job. If I was going to live forever, I'd rather do it in a nice house than in an alley. "Do you think?" I asked her, wondering if I could make money doing something I loved. It almost didn't seem fair.

Ms. Cartwright set down the photo when another woman began looking over the pictures. Recognizing her, I pointed hers out. Her ooh of delight made me smile, and she lingered before going to pay for it, laughing at pictures of her neighbors.

"I'll talk to the counselor and get you into my advanced class," Ms. Cartwright said to bring my attention back. "You'll be a senior this year, right?"

A thrill ran through me. Senior. I liked the sound of that. "Okay," I said. "You convinced me." I was happier being myself—purple hair, loud music, dead, and everything—than trying to fit in with the Amys. And I didn't think that Josh would dump me just because I wasn't in the cool crowd. Not that we really were anything.

She nodded, sliding down to take the photo of Josh, one of the first to have printed out. "Another one of Josh?" she said, smiling. "Wow, you did good here. Did you take this from the bleachers?" I nodded, and she murmured, "Steady hand. Too bad about the glint of sun in the picture. Funny. Those don't usually show up when the sun is at that angle." She frowned, bringing the picture to her nose. "Something about this one makes me uneasy. The pinch of his eyes, perhaps . . ." Her shoulders lifted and fell. "It might be the crows in the background. My grandmother would chase them off her roof all the time. She hated crows."

My face stiffened. *Crows?*

Ms. Cartwright set the photo down. "You did great today, Madison," she said with a smile. "People have been giving more than the requested donation. You brought in over two hundred dollars."

There hadn't been any crows at the track—had there? Grace had been right there with Josh. I'd seen her.

"Better than the dunk tank," Ms. Cartwright was saying. "Howard will be disappointed. He's usually the big draw. Why don't you call it a day?" she suggested. "Go enjoy yourself. They're about to read the totals. You should find Josh and stick around for the party. There will be dancing. . . ."

She gave me a final smile and was pulled away by a nervous

woman holding a handful of tickets. I hardly noticed her leaving, and I snatched up the last picture I'd taken of Josh. Those weren't crows in the background; they were black wings. They were in the distance above the tree line, but that was what they were.

Frantic, I looked out from under the tent to search the line the trees made with the sky. Nothing. I could only see a small slice of heaven. Something must be wrong. Grace was supposed to be watching him, but there were black wings, and where there were black wings, there were reapers. Or Kairos. If he was here, I'd never know it. Grace's job was to protect Josh, not tell me when there was trouble.

In a surge of motion, I disconnected my camera from the printer. The pictures were already in the queue, and after making sure there was enough paper in the hopper, I slipped out under the ropes at the back of the tent. I had to find Josh.

Nine

The people around me turned from beautiful representations of
life to annoying obstacles, and I dodged through them trying
to phone Josh and scan the skies at the same time. "Must be
still running," I muttered when I got no answer, and I shoved
my phone into a back pocket. I made better progress that way,
but the occasional hail from some of the same people I'd taken
pictures of earlier slowed me down as I begged off taking any
new ones.

The sun was hot, but being dead had its advantages, and I
wasn't even sweating when I finally got back to the track. Heat
had pushed almost all the watchers to the nearby shade, and
I spotted Josh quickly. He was running just as when I'd left
him, looking strong and ready to go another lap or two. Relief
unclenched my jaw, but it tightened again when I scanned the

line of trees. Black wings. At least six.

"Crap," I whispered, climbing up onto the chain-link fence between the bleachers and the track to try to get Josh's attention. The black wings were distant, but they were there. It was as if they were confused. Finally Josh spotted me, and I frantically waved.

Immediately he gestured for a runner to come out to take his place and slowed to a walk. Breathing heavily, he caught the bottled water someone threw at him and headed my way.

"That's sixteen laps total!" a thick-looking man called, squinting from under a clip-on umbrella. "Good job, Josh. Are you coming to the Low D with the rest of the track team? Pizza's on me."

Josh searched my concerned expression, then waved him off. "No, thanks!" he called. "I gotta go." And the man went back to his clipboard. From the sidelines, Amy frowned, watching us with a hand on a hip. Beside her was a blond girl dressed exactly like her.

"What's up?" Josh said as I opened the latch to the gate and he came through. "You look like you've seen a ghost."

"Very funny. Ha-ha," I said, tugging him toward the parking lot. If Kairos was around, this was not the place to meet him. "Look at this," I said, handing him his picture.

A smile came over his face. "Look at the sweat on me! Is that Grace?"

From above us came a tiny giggle, and I glanced up, to be

blinded by the sun. Blinking, I stumbled over to the pile of bags. "Check out the horizon," I suggested as my sight cleared, "not how good you look."

"Black wings?" he said.

"They're not crows," I said, ducking when Grace hovered close to the photo to see.

"It's not my fault," Grace said as Josh started to shove stuff into his bag. "I've been with him all day," she protested. "See, that's me in the photograph. And besides, they haven't gotten any closer. Much."

Josh zipped up his gym bag and straightened, shooting nervous glances at the tree line and the waiting black wings. "You knew they were there?" I questioned her, and the glow of her light brightened.

"Well, yeah. They've been there all along." Grace's tinkling voice sounded sarcastic. "Slowly circling in. It's as if a reaper is about, but not sure where they're going."

I looked at Josh, afraid and almost guilty. What was I doing enjoying myself, hiding among my neighbors like an ostrich? I should be in a back alley facing down this creep. The fact that Grace thought going invisible was dangerous shouldn't have stopped me.

"We gotta go," I said, and after glancing at his teammates, Josh nodded. His face was pale, and together we headed for the exit. "Grace, if you try to stop us, I swear I'm going to take your name away."

She was silent, and tension wound its way through my gut, worsening when we found the midway and the slowly milling people. We had to go past the bandstand to reach the parking lot, and it had gotten crowded as everyone was congregating to hear the totals. The middle school band was trying to organize, and between the parents waving for their kids' attention and the officials bringing in the last numbers, getting through the crowd was impossible.

There can't be this many people in all of Three Rivers, I thought sourly, then jerked to a halt to avoid running into a stroller when Josh caught my elbow. There was no way to get through this fast. Giving him a mirthless smile, I slowed down.

"Maybe the black wings can't find us among everyone," Josh said.

I nodded. "Maybe," I said, remembering the people whose lives I had stolen today. I'd never considered I might endanger them simply by walking among them, but I probably had. "I'm thinking Kairos is looking for us with his eyes, since he can't track our auras."

From above, Grace said, "It's not Kairos, and reapers don't hunt people with their eyes. It takes too long and they make mistakes. You all look alike to them, especially to dark reapers."

"It *is* Kairos, and I don't think he cares if he makes a mistake," I protested. "All bets are off, Grace. He wants his amulet back, and he doesn't want anyone else to know he's lost it."

Josh's lips pressed together, and he angled for an opening in the crowd. "I can only hear half this conversation," he complained. "Maybe someone else is getting scythed," he suggested.

"They've been hanging on the horizon for hours," Grace said as we worked around the last of the watchers. "It would have happened by now and the black wings would be gone."

"Grace says if it was a normal scythe, it would have happened by now," I said for Josh's benefit. "I still think it's Kairos looking for us."

We dodged around a last group of people. Finally the way was clear. Leaving the band to start up an enthusiastic version of "Louie, Louie," we jogged to the parking lot, loaded down with our stuff. I relaxed somewhat when we reached it with its tired yellow balloons hanging from sticks marking the borders. Hesitating like a deer at the edge of the woods, I looked up and down the rows. Where had Josh parked?

"There," Josh said, pointing to the shade tree as if having read my mind, and we broke into a fast pace, hearing the cheer when the band stopped and Ms. Cartwright's voice come over the loudspeaker to thank everyone for coming. I sighed when the back of his truck became visible from around a big-butt van. But my relief turned to irritation when I noticed who was waiting for us.

"How did they get here before us?" I said. Amy was in the truck's bed, elbows on the top of the cab, trying to look sexy in her running shorts. That white bandage across her nose killed the effect. Parker stood by the tailgate, shuffling uneasily, and Len was leaning against the front door with his arms crossed, as if he wanted to start some trouble. My hands fisted. I didn't have time for this.

"Holy sweet seraph nubs," Grace muttered. "This has not been my day."

From the truck bed, Amy called out, "Hi, Madison, sweetie."

It was mocking, and the skin around Josh's mouth was tight as he fished out his keys from his gym bag. "Get off my truck," he said shortly.

Amy opened her mouth again, and I blurted, "Hi, Amy. What did you do to your nose?"

Turning pink in embarrassment, she said coyly, "Is that a new outfit? You're as cute as my little sister in those tights."

The way she said it made it sound like I was three, and I fumed, thinking I might make a hundred copies of the shot with her mouth open catching flies and her nose swollen and blue—then post them in the high school's halls.

Len hadn't moved, and Josh stepped closer. "Why don't you grow up?" he said tightly.

Seeing the picture in Josh's grip, Len leaned forward. "Let me see," he said, grabbing it, and Amy snatched it in turn.

"Oh, isn't that precious?" she mocked. "How many did you take of him, sweetie?"

My lips pressed together, but a soft rustle of leaves drew my attention up to see a black wing ghost overhead and move on. Eyes wide, I felt the whisper of my heart start up. *Not here. Not now!*

Amy must have thought I was afraid of her, because she jumped from the truck and sashayed closer. "The team's going to the Low D, Josh," she said. "Everyone will be there. You're coming, right?"

Her unspoken "you, but not her" was obvious, making me angry. Josh took the photo back and reached beyond Len for the truck's handle. He opened it with a yank hard enough to send Len stumbling forward. "No," he said as he tucked the photo on the dash and shoved his bag under the seat. "Why don't you go take a shower, Amy? You're sweating like a pig."

Her mouth dropped open, and I snickered loud enough for her to hear.

Len had tried to make his lurch look like it was planned, but he had lost face and he knew it. Even his laugh didn't help. "Come on," he said as he put his hands in his pockets and started to move away. "I'm not wasting any more time here. Let's go. Parker?"

Amy draped an arm over Parker's shoulders to lead him away. He looked like he wanted to say something, but all he did was shrug when Josh met his eyes. Josh shrugged back.

I tried to get my heart stopped as Amy and Parker walked between Josh and me, and I forced my hands to unclench. They were three cars away when Amy called out to someone else, and they angled that way. In the distance, the band started up again, loud and enthusiastic.

Josh looked pissed. His neck was red as he got into the truck and started the engine.

Anxious to be away, I turned to go around the back of the truck, jerking to a halt when a lithe shape dropped out of the tree and into my way. My breath hissed in. Nakita.

"You?" I stammered, trying to realign my thoughts. But it made sense. Nakita was the only dark reaper who would be able to recognize me by sight—and since she knew I had Kairos's amulet, Kairos had nothing to lose by sending her after me.

"I told you it was a reaper!" Grace shrilled. "Get out of here, Madison!"

Nakita took a step forward, eyeing the angel. Her smile deepened. "I think Ron *wants* your soul destroyed. He left a first-sphere to watch you? She's not capable of stopping me."

I stumbled back. "Josh! It's a reaper!" I shouted, and I heard his truck creak as he got out.

With a soft, confident smile, Nakita took off her sunglasses and threw them aside. She was wearing long pants and a skin-tight top, all white. A gold belt hung about her hips, and she sported a white, luminescent duster, its hem dragging on the matted grass. The gem on her drawn blade glinted a rich, violet hue, matching the amulet around her neck. Death was walking—looking for me. "Hello, Madison," she said, naming me as she tossed her long black hair back. "You're a hard soul to find."

I backed up, gripping my camera like it might help me. Crap, where was Barnabas when I needed him? I could not claim Nakita's amulet because she was a reaper—how was I supposed to do this? I had to figure out a way to take it from her. But how? I had to do it fast.

Josh was suddenly beside me, looking scared but determined. Grace hovered over us. I heard a rustle from the tree—black wings. "Do it!" Josh whispered intently.

I might as well try and see what happened. If I didn't, Josh was dead. I had nothing to lose. Handing him my camera, I took a deep breath to bring the mental image of my amulet into my mind and wiped every line I could see that was connecting me to the present. I staggered, almost falling from the dizzying sensation of going insubstantial. Grace was abruptly visible, and Josh was backing slowly away. In my grip was my amulet, but it felt like I didn't really have it. Grace was looking right at me, her expression scared. A little voice in me was saying that something wasn't right, but I didn't have the time to think about it, and I reached for Nakita's amulet.

"Madison, no!" Grace shouted, but it was too late.

"Hey!" I yelped when Nakita casually snatched my wrist with her free hand. "You're not supposed to be able to see me," I said stupidly, shocked as I looked up at her.

Josh was white-faced, clearly seeing me as well. I didn't

understand! I could see my amulet in my mind's eye, the threads being cut as they shifted from future to present, but I was visible!

Her full lips curved up in a smile, and Nakita jerked me closer, wrapping her arm around my neck and pinning my back to her. "I don't know what you're trying to do, but stop drawing on my amulet, you little succubus!"

Her *amulet?* I thought, then realized what had happened. Just as when I'd been dead in the morgue and Barnabas's amulet had tied me to the present, so was Nakita's now. *Dumb, dumb, dumb!* I berated myself. I might be able to see Grace, but I wasn't entirely invisible. *Damn it!*

Immediately I stopped destroying the threads, and Grace became a hazy ball of light. Nakita still had me, and I tried to get out from her hold, to no avail.

"Let her go!" Josh shouted as he jumped at us.

God, no!

Nakita ducked back out of Josh's swing, yanking me off balance. Before I could gain my footing, she kicked out, hitting him in his solar plexus. Josh flew back, an ugly noise escaping him as he fell to his knees beside my abandoned camera and tried to breathe. His eyes were wide, and sweat plastered his hair to his face. Nakita was a lot stronger than she looked.

"Okay. You got me. Leave him alone," I said breathlessly as I eyed first her sword, then her amulet, inches from me.

"Kairos wants to see you," she said, her pale blue eyes looking cold. "Apparently there is a small matter about bringing your soul and body and my scythe together."

Crap, I thought, trying to twist away. This was so not good. "Promise me you'll leave Josh alone," I said, reaching up past her arm at my throat until my fingertips brushed the cool stone about her neck. Nothing happened. If I could touch it, I could take it. As long as I didn't claim it, I'd be okay. She smiled and shifted me away so that my fingertips slipped off.

"Your friend dies first," she said. "Kairos is two days older than he was last week, and he's cranky."

They got me, and she's going to scythe Josh anyway? I thought. Then I gasped again when Nakita shoved me and I went flying forward, arms and legs flailing. I hit the ground hard beside Josh. My gaze moved to the trees, and I reached to help Josh up, terrified at the dripping black sheets I saw. Black wings were flying through the branches and circling the tree. They could strip my soul and destroy me utterly. What was bringing them in? Both my amulet and Grace were hiding our auras! Weren't they?

I looked up to see Nakita grinning, showing her perfect teeth. The sharp edge of her blade glinted, and when she lunged for Josh, I rolled, slamming into her legs. Shrieking, she fell on me. I scrambled to get her amulet, and she shoved me off, spinning to stand.

"Madison, get the blazes out of the way!" Grace cried.

Josh groaned. I found my feet, looking for him. He was on his back, staring upward. Nakita's blade was bared and gleaming in a shaft of light.

"Josh!" I shouted, and I almost cried in relief when he moved to roll over and get his arms under himself. He wasn't dead. *But he's hurt. Did she cut him?*

Nakita suddenly frowned, clearly not happy. A black wing flew between Josh and me, and my fear grew so heady I could almost taste it. They were getting bolder. I couldn't let them touch him. Grace dropped down. I tensed when she met one, and it vanished in a sparkle of sideways light. I would have cheered, but another took its place.

"Kairos told me how you stole his amulet," Nakita said, and my attention rose to her as she stood by the truck with her blade bared. "That was a mistake. It's not only going to end your life but destroy your soul. The boy is done for. Time to go."

Seeing Nakita smile as the slight breeze shifted her long hair, I felt my fear turn to anger: anger that she thought I'd go meekly to my end, anger that she had hurt Josh, anger that she was stronger than me, and anger that everything I'd learned yesterday meant nothing. "I'd like to see you try to take me," I said, falling into a half crouch.

Nakita laughed, her voice setting the last black wings into the air. "You don't have a choice. It's fate," she said, the happy band music in the background a stark contrast to her threats. "You're not supposed to have that stone. You're supposed to be dead. And with you gone, we can all go back to the way things were. The way they have been for millennia."

"Except I'll be dead," I said, and she shrugged.

"You can always just give me the stone right now," she said, slim hand extended.

"Don't think so," I said, and her eyes narrowed.

Grace dropped down beside me, and I waved her away. "Stay with Josh!" I demanded.

"The black wings aren't after him," she protested. "They're after you! Madison, don't go invisible anymore. You're cracking your amulet. It's breaking. I told you it was dangerous. It's only Nakita's amulet keeping them off you now."

It's only Nakita's amulet that's keeping me from going misty and this lame plan of mine from working, I thought, then hesitated. If her amulet was tying me to the present, then why couldn't I sever my ties to Nakita's amulet as well as my own?

"Madison, don't!" Grace said, as if knowing what I was going to do.

"Stay with Josh," I insisted, and her glow redoubled in frustration.

Nakita came at me and I backpedaled, scrambling for the time and space to figure out how to disconnect myself from her amulet. I couldn't feel a connection, but it had to be there. And I couldn't fight her and find it at the same time.

I looked to Josh kneeling on the ground with his head bowed. I thought of my dad and how I wanted to see him again. I thought of the people living their lives, moment by beautiful moment, captured by my camera, ignorant of the gift they'd been given. I wasn't ready to leave. I had to find a way to make this work, to make a stronger connection between Nakita's amulet and myself so that I could break it—and I had to do it without claiming the deadly thing.

Closing my eyes and praying I wasn't making a mistake, I let her touch me.

I stiffened when her hand pinched my shoulder. Willing myself into my unconscious, I let the existence of my amulet fill my mental sight. Beside it was another, much weaker presence. Nakita's amulet held far fewer threads to me, but as I watched, the number grew, making me more solid, more real. *More dead,* I thought, trying to cut the lines between us, and only succeeding in wiping out the lines from me to my amulet.

Nakita felt it and jerked, but her hand was still on me and I wasn't invisible. I couldn't cut the lines from her amulet to me without taking control of it, and I couldn't take control of it unless I claimed it. Do that, and I'd be blown to dust. *But her sword,* I thought suddenly. It was *made* from her amulet. A direct connection to it. Maybe if I worked through that . . .

Nakita's sound of surprise pulled my eyes open. Grace was above Josh, bathing him in a haze of light. She was beautiful and savage, a harsh beauty that hurt to look at. And she was crying. Crying for me. I tried to tell her it would be okay, but I couldn't think of the words.

Something fell on me, sending me staggering. I would have fallen if not for Nakita holding me up. I met her eyes, and they widened. Her lips opened, and horror crossed her face.

Unexpected and overwhelming pain jerked me stiff. I fell to a knee when Nakita shoved me away. In sudden terror, I realized what it was. A black wing. A black wing had found me.

Cold so deep it felt like fire pushed from my spine and into my mind. I gasped, unable to scream. It wasn't death. It was the sensation of never having existed, of never being. The black wing was taking my memories and leaving emptiness in its place. It was destroying me, stripping my past away, moment by moment.

Instinct pushed me backward to the earth. Frantic with pain, I tried to scrape the black wing off, writhing. I reached to pull it free, but the cold sheet hung like a second, sucking skin. It was eating my soul, burning where I touched it with my hands!

I got to my feet, agony in every move. I stood, staggering as another fell on me. Shocked, I could do nothing. The pain had shifted me back to being visible—I couldn't even see my amulet, much less the lines of connection—and, wobbling, I looked at Nakita.

I had failed. I'd made a mistake, and I was going to die. Clever, beautiful Nakita had gained my end and the stone with no trouble at all. If I did nothing, I was going to be eaten out of existence. I should be happy. I'd had an extra summer of life. But it wasn't enough, and I refused my end even as I saw it. All

I needed was her damned sword. It connected directly with her amulet, and through it, I was sure I could sever the ties it was making to me.

"You may be a dark reaper," I said as my limbs seemed to go numb, "but you don't know crap about human determination."

She blinked, eyes wide and confused. Gritting my teeth, I went for her.

Two years of practice kicked in, and I planted my left foot on the ground beside her right, then spun to stand sideways next to her, my right elbow swinging with all my momentum toward her middle. I hit Nakita's gut hard. She bent forward, muscles seizing.

Her blade hung slack, and I grabbed it above her fingers. It was mine and hers both. In my mind's eye, I could see our two amulets and all the lines holding me to the now.

Realizing I was trying to take it, Nakita put her hand above mine that was gripping her sword. We both held it. I had to go misty. The sword would come with me if I did. But I hurt.

If I couldn't do this, Josh would die. I wouldn't let him die just because I was afraid of pain. The decision was easy.

My hand ached under the angel's grip. I gave in to the pain. I let it wash through me and away, leaving me scoured clean of everything but my will. Euphoria rose, a false high as my mind tried to protect itself. Exhilarated and powerful, I exhaled, blowing on the ties connecting me to the present—and with the breath of my will, all of them shriveled like silk threads in flame. Her sword was mine.

"No!" Nakita shouted, pulling back as she felt her blade go invisible with me. I was the mist, and she couldn't hold me, but she lunged as if she could. Instinct brought my hand up, and the reaper passed right through me, her amulet blazing like a violet flame.

Nakita's face went wonder-struck, and her mouth opened in a silent scream. It was as if time slowed, and I held my breath so as not to breathe her in. I started to crumple, feeling her cold anger, tasting her frustration, seeing in my mind Kairos standing on a black tile floor in the sun and telling her I was a threat to seraph will and sending her secretly after me. For an instant, I was her. I was Nakita—and she was me.

The black wings attached to me felt her too. And they found something better to eat than my paltry seventeen years of memory.

Nakita screamed in agony as the black wings let go of me and cleaved to her instead. Pain lifted from me as they parted from my soul, embedding themselves inside the reaper as she passed through me.

I hit the ground, and the shock broke my mental hold on the amulets. Lines burst into existence, two stones tying me to the present. I was again solid. Nakita stood above me, stiff with pain. In my hand was not her sword, but her amulet. By taking one, I'd taken both.

Her voice pitched high in agony, Nakita dropped to kneel upon the ground. Her white wings shimmered into existence, stretching to the high branches. I scuttled backward to Josh, frightened. Josh looked up, one hand to his middle as he watched, shaking as Grace again became a glowing ball of light above us.

A third piercing scream came from Nakita. It didn't sound human, and fear iced my veins. She had black wings *inside* her. I stared, horrified, as I realized what I'd done. But I hadn't known. I hadn't known!

Her wings and back arched again in what must have been horrible pain, and her wail cut off with a frightening suddenness as, with a downward thrust of wings, she vanished. Dirt and grass clippings flew, and I cowered.

"Madison," Grace said, her terrified voice clear over the noise of the middle school band. "Get in the truck. Get Josh and get in the truck."

Nakita was gone, but the black wings were still swarming. There were hundreds of them. I was solid, and Grace was with us, but they were not dissipating. "Josh," I panted, feeling weary and insubstantial. Stumbling, I helped him up, Nakita's amulet wrapped around my wrist. Lurching, I snagged my camera, forgotten on the ground. The truck door was open, and I shoved him in, making him slide across to the passenger side. It was still running, and I thanked God for small favors.

"Is Josh okay?" I panted as I slammed the door shut. The

hard gearshift felt like it was going right through to my bones. "Did she hit him?"

"It wasn't a clean strike," Grace said. "I would have stopped her entirely, but you got in the way. His soul is hanging by a thread. Get out of here. I can't stop a concentrated effort if they attack together. I'm hiding you, but two got a taste of you, and the others sense that. Don't go invisible again. Madison, *don't go invisible*! You're cracking your amulet a little more every time you do."

I was shaking as I backed the truck up and then put it into forward gear. Josh was slumped against the passenger door. *Don't go invisible.* Grace had said that before. That it drew the black wings in. But I hadn't had a choice.

"Josh?" I said as we found the pavement and I slowed to an infuriating crawl to avoid the people just now starting to abandon the park. "Josh, talk to me." I looked behind me, but it was as if no one had heard Nakita scream. No one had seen a winged angel arched in pain in a terrible beauty under the trees.

I reached to shake him, and he groaned. "Hospital," he whispered. "Madison, I feel like I'm dying. Get me there. Please."

Fear struck me. I jostled out onto the main road, and then I floored it. Horns blew, and I turned the hazard lights on, for what good they would do.

When my dad found out about this, he was going to kill me. Again.

Ten

The smell of rubbing alcohol and adhesive drifted out from the sterile white hallway and into the brown-and-taupe emergency waiting room. It was quiet now but for a woman with a fussy baby on her lap, and I hunched over my knees and rubbed my elbow, remembering what it had felt like when I'd hit Nakita. I was tired, weary of waiting to hear something. The mom had a little boy with her too, who was busy causing trouble and probably mad that his little sister was getting all the attention.

Harried, the woman was giving me dirty looks as she filled out paperwork to get her feverish baby girl looked at. She'd been here when I'd blown in, but an unconscious person gets treatment before a colicky baby. Though some of the rush might have been caused by me yelling at the emergency people.

I hadn't shut up until a cop, who had apparently been following me, had come in. I swear, I hadn't seen her in my rearview mirror. Maybe I'd been going too fast, but it had taken only eight minutes to get here.

Eight terrifying minutes in which I thought Josh was going to die.

My feet scuffed the flat carpet, and I slumped into the cushions as I glanced at the officer talking to the nurse in a pink lab coat. The young-looking cop had my license, which meant my dad was probably on his way. I'd tried to call but had been unable to bring myself to leave a message other than that I was okay and that I was at the hospital with Josh.

The sight of the nurse made my gut cramp in worry. Josh had been whisked away after I'd said he'd collapsed at the track. This woman in her pink lab coat was the first medical person I'd seen since, and she wasn't telling me anything. Stupid privacy laws.

At least Grace was with him, though the angel wasn't happy. Actually, she was royally P.O.'ed, and I think they almost checked me in for observation when I'd had a hushed argument with her until she capitulated. He was unconscious and I wasn't, so he needed her. Duh.

The cop's voice rose, and I grew nervous when they looked my way. The two women said something in parting; the nurse went down the hall, and the cop came to me. I couldn't remember the name she had given to me in our first discussion, but her badge said B Levy. B for Betty? Bea? Barbie? Nah. Not with that pistol on her hip.

Officer Levy stopped a shade too close for my comfort, her no-nonsense shoes rocking slightly on the carpet as she halted. My eyes traveled up her pressed pants, belt, weapon secured in a snapped holster, starched shirt, badge, and finally to her face. She didn't look old enough to have been a cop for long, and it irritated me that her expression was trying for parental concern. Right, like she had kids? Don't think so.

She had a nice face, though, with short, sandy-blond hair and hazel eyes, suntanned and showing only worry wrinkles. She wasn't saying anything, and when she arched her eyebrows, I looked away. She could give me a ticket for reckless driving and failure to stop, but what traffic-school, goody-two-shoes Scrooge would press charges for that when I was going to the hospital with an injured friend?

"Josh has stabilized," she said, and my gaze darted up, surprised.

"Thank you," I whispered, and my shoulders eased. I hadn't known they were tense.

"They had an ambulance at the carnival," the officer said as she took the seat beside me, sighing when the weight left her feet and she ran a hand over her hair. She looked too spunky to be a cop. I hated it when people called me spunky, but that's what she looked like: fun, energetic, and someone who'd push the limits for a little excitement.

"Why didn't you take him there instead of endangering the entire town?" she added. She wasn't anything like the cops who'd brought me home after I broke curfew during a Category 1 hurricane at my mom's house. Talk about drama.

"I didn't know there was an ambulance," I admitted, but what was I going to tell her? That a dark reaper had tried to kill Josh and he needed major medical attention?

The officer chuckled. "You drive pretty well," she said, and I gave her a sour smile.

"Thanks." I quit rubbing my elbow where I'd hit Nakita when she looked at it, clasping my hands together instead. Officer Levy sat up straighter, and I sighed. *Here comes the lecture.*

"I've called your parents," she said, and I turned to her, alarmed.

"You called my mom?" I asked, really worried. She would flip out.

"No. Your dad. You have a worrisome record, Madison, for someone your age."

My record didn't bother me, since it wasn't anything bad like shoplifting or armed robbery. Just breaking curfew and loitering. Whoo-hoo! Big freaking hairy deal. Relieved, I slumped into the chair. "What was I supposed to do, Officer Levy?" I asked, my expression begging for understanding. "What would you have done? So I drove a little fast to get Josh to the hospital. I was scared, okay? I thought he was dying."

The woman's eyebrows rose. "I would have called for help

and stayed with the victim until it arrived. You generally don't die from heatstroke."

"If it was heatstroke, they would've let me see him by now," I said, and she made a soft noise of agreement. The silence grew, and thinking she was waiting for me to say something, I offered a hesitant, "I'll remember that next time. Call for help. Stay with the victim." But there was no one on earth who could have helped me. Maybe I shouldn't have given Grace any orders. It seemed to have wiped out whatever orders Ron had left with her, including going to get him if there was trouble she couldn't handle.

Officer Levy got to her feet so she could look stern again. "I'm hoping there won't be a next time," she said as she handed me my license. "Don't leave until I have a chance to talk to your dad."

"Okay." I took the laminated card, glad she didn't want me to go fill out a report or anything. "Thank you."

Officer Levy hesitated. "Are you sure you don't want to tell me anything else?"

Hiding my alarm, I looked steadily up at her. "No. Why?"

Her gaze remained fixed on mine. "You have grass in your hair and dirt on your tights."

My gaze wavered, and I refused to look at my legs. *Damn it!*

"Was there a fight?" she asked, her eyes narrowing. "Who else was involved?"

Looking away, I shrugged.

Officer Levy sighed. "I know it's hard to fit in at a new school, but if there was a fight, I need to know. You're not a snitch."

"Josh didn't get into a fight," I said. "He collapsed." I could have lied and told her I fell down and got dirty while catching him, but why bother?

She just looked at me, and I stared back. Finally she pressed her lips together, and with another one of her small noises, she walked over to the receptionist. Officer Levy would probably stay until she could talk to Josh's parents. I hoped I'd be out of here before they showed up. Josh was a good guy, and I knew they'd take one look at my purple hair and earrings and label me not good enough for their little boy, thinking someone like Amy was better.

I snorted, wondering when I had started thinking of Josh as boyfriend material. We'd spent two afternoons together. Admittedly they were fight-for-your-life afternoons—which would probably only convince him we were *not* couple material.

My gaze lifted to peer through the windows to Josh's truck. I'd stashed the amulet under the front seat when we'd gotten clear of the black wings. I didn't think Nakita would be coming back, but Kairos might, and if he did, he'd know Nakita's amulet's resonance. The sound of her screaming had been awful, and I stifled a shiver at the thought of the black wings heavy on me, like a blanket of cold acid eating my memories—my life.

Brow pinched, I wondered what I'd lost. The fact that they'd cleaved to Nakita instead had been a shock. It was horrifying, and I hoped she was all right—even if she'd been trying to kill me.

A familiar form in jeans and a T-shirt moving past the windows caught my attention, and I sat up, jaw dropping as Barnabas waited impatiently for the automatic door to open. "Where have you been?" I demanded when he came in with a gust of air that made his gray duster billow.

"I leave for one day—" he started, his dark eyes cross.

"And it all goes to Hades," I said as I stood, not wanting him to have the high ground. "Yeah. I was here dealing with it. I've been evading Kairos and Nakita since yesterday!" I said with hushed forcefulness.

"Nakita?" he asked, clearly not listening to everything I said.

"Yes, Nakita," I shot back, worried. She'd left in a lot of pain. Angels shouldn't be in pain, even dark reapers.

Barnabas sat on the edge of a seat across from me and ran a hand over his frizzy brown hair to tame it somewhat. For a reaper, he looked innocent. Especially in the rock-band shirt he had on. "It *was* you?" he said, and I sat back down beside him. "The songs between heaven and earth say that she was hurt in battle. Naturally Ron thought of you and sent me to check. He, uh, wants to talk to you."

I bet. Miserable, I sat perfectly straight in my chair. Songs between heaven and earth? I bet that beat CNN with a stick.

Barnabas looked askance at me. "What happened? I can't believe you took her amulet. Madison, you have to stop doing that. Where's your guardian angel? We never heard from her that there was trouble."

"That might be my fault," I said softly. "I told her to protect Josh, so she didn't leave to get you. Don't be mad at her. I told her to do it."

"Josh?" Barnabas jerked upright. "The guardian angel is supposed to be with you!"

He looked shocked, and I shrugged. "I'm conscious. Josh isn't. Easy choice."

"She's supposed to be with you!" he exclaimed again.

I made an exasperated noise. "I told her to watch him. She saved his life twice now. Kairos tried to kill him yesterday. What was I supposed to do? Let him? I was fine." *Until the black wings found me. And Grace said I'd cracked my amulet. Freaking fantastic.*

Barnabas continued to stare at me in disbelief. "She left you," he stated.

Cripes! Is he still on that? "Not by her choice," I said, hoping I hadn't gotten Grace into trouble. "She wasn't happy about it." I hesitated, looking down the long white hallway. "Nakita tried to kill Josh. I think she nicked him. Will he be okay?"

"I don't know." Barnabas glanced at the receptionist and the cop, then leaned back with his arms crossed over his chest.

"What did you do to Nakita? Taking her amulet would only limit her skills and make her angry, not catatonic."

Nakita is catatonic? Barnabas was staring at me, and I was starting to think I'd done something really wrong. Sure, she was a dark reaper, but leaving black wings inside her was awful. Even if it had been an accident. "I had to get her to leave," I said, pitching my voice barely above a whisper when Officer Levy looked at us. "I did the best I could. It's not like I was able to touch your thoughts," I finished bitterly.

Barnabas's face grew darker. "Ron left you a guardian angel," he said, leaning forward to hunch over his knees. "You should have been okay."

"Yeah?" It was hard, but I managed to not yell the word. Two days of fear was coming out as anger, and I couldn't help it. "Nakita said he left me a *first-sphere* guardian angel. I like her and all, but she's not powerful enough to protect me against a concentrated attack, and Ron knows it."

Barnabas's anger vanished in surprise and he drew back, watching the woman and her two kids as they were escorted into a room. The nurse who'd called them told Officer Levy she could come back as well, and taking that as a good sign, I found a modicum of control. I watched Barnabas's fingers unclench, thinking they looked a shade too long for a human's.

"Josh knows you're dead?" he asked, and I nodded, unable to look from the carpet. I shouldn't have gotten him involved, but choice vanished when black wings began following him.

"I had to tell him," I said. "Black wings were tracking him, but as long as I was with him, he was okay. I made my angel stay with him last night. He wouldn't have lived through it otherwise." And now he was in the hospital. *Way to go, Madison.*

A jump of shadows caught my attention, and I pulled my head up to find Ron simply standing there, looking almost sad with his hands clasped before him. The sun coming in shone on his tight, graying curls, and his eyes were a grayish blue as they took in my yellow tights and purple skirt. His eyes had been brown yesterday. I didn't think gray eyes were a good sign. Every time I saw them, he was upset with me.

"Madison," he said, and the amount of weary fatigue in the sound of my name scared me.

"I'm sorry," I said, frightened.

"I know you are." He glanced at the empty reception desk before he approached, his slippers silent on the carpet. "It's been over two thousand years since an angel has returned from battle without a blade and unconscious. Do you have any idea what it takes to do that?"

Miserable, I shrank back into the thin cushions. "Black wings stuck in her?" I offered hesitantly. *God help me, but it was an accident!*

Ron's intake of breath was loud, and Barnabas made a surprised-sounding noise. I couldn't look up, afraid of what I might find.

"How did Nakita get black wings inside of her?" Ron asked,

each word slow and precise.

My head came up and I found Ron's expression one of sadness. "I, uh, accidentally put them there?" I said, hating the way my voice went up at the end.

"Excuse me?" Ron said, the phrase sounding odd coming from him.

Barnabas was shaking his head. "That's impossible. Black wings can't hurt reapers. She must be confused as to what really happened."

That was insulting, and I made a huff of sound. "I am not. I know what happened," I said, finding the words easier to say than I thought they would be. "Grace said that when I went invisible, I was dissociating from my amulet. That's what drew the black wings in, and when Nakita fell through me, the black wings stuck to her instead."

"Grace?" Ron asked, his round face tight with worry. "Who's Grace?" His expression became pained. "You named her? Madison, you didn't name your guardian angel, did you?"

Compared to leaving black wings inside an angel to eat her from the inside out, naming Grace seemed like a small thing. "I was breaking the lines of connection to my amulet only in the present, not the ones pulling me to the future," I explained, trying to make myself sound less foolish than I felt, and I could almost see Ron switch mental gears to understand what I was saying. At least, I think that's why he suddenly looked horrified.

Barnabas, though, was less than impressed. "What does that have to do with black wings?" he asked.

"Nakita was going to reap Josh, even though she had me. I couldn't get her scythe away from her unless I went invisible. I had to find some way to protect myself, and neither of you were around," I said, pleading for understanding. "I didn't know the black wings would stick to her instead. She's a reaper! Black wings aren't supposed to hurt reapers!"

Ron's head was going back and forth in denial. "That's not how to go invisible. Madison, you weren't bending light around you; you were breaking your connection to your amulet, as if you weren't really wearing it. Dead with no connection to life. A walking soul without a body. No wonder you brought in black wings. They were . . . on you?"

Grace had said it was dangerous. I should've listened to her. "Nakita was going to kill Josh and take me to Kairos. I thought if I swiped her sword, she at least couldn't kill Josh. But when I went invisible to take her amulet, two black wings fell on me." Fear made me shiver. "It hurt. I think I lost something of myself." I paused as the memory of them eating my past rose anew. I unclenched my hands as I thought about Nakita and what it must be like to have two of those things inside her. "It really hurt, Ron. I went invisible again to try to get her sword away, and they sort of stuck to her when she fell through me." I looked up, my vision swimming. "I only wanted her to go away," I finished miserably. Damn it, I wasn't going to cry.

Barnabas had pulled back like I was a snake. "What about Nakita's amulet?" he asked. "How come her amulet didn't keep you grounded?"

"Because I cut those ties too," I said. "I claimed her sword, not her amulet, and it gave me enough control to break the ties without frying me."

Barnabas stood, his face pale. "Ron," he said, looking at me. "She broke the hold Nakita's amulet had on her while the reaper was still wearing it! How much proof do you need? I believe in choice, as do you, but this is wrong! Look at what's happened. Madison is—"

"Fine." Ron took up my hands and jerked my attention from Barnabas. His round face was smiling confidently, but his eyes were deathly worried. "She's fine."

"Nakita said you drew a first-sphere to watch her," Barnabas interrupted, anger coloring his face. "It's clear why. You know this is a mistake. It's wrong, and you know it!"

The older man glared at Barnabas, his grip on me tightening. "I do *not* have to explain myself to *you*. I called for a first-sphere because chances were slim anything would happen, and I didn't want to advertise that anything was wrong."

"Wrong." Barnabas faced him squarely, and Ron's expression went ugly. "You admit it, then."

"Barnabas, will you shut up!" the master of time exclaimed, and Barnabas dropped his head, frustrated. I sat there, stunned. It was the second time I'd seen Ron curtail Barnabas's words, first at the school parking lot, and then here. Something wasn't right. What had I done?

"Ron," I said, scared, "I'm sorry. I was only trying to keep Josh and myself safe. She nicked him. Is he going to be okay?"

The timekeeper seemed to notice for the first time where he was. Giving me an unhappy look, he shook his head, sending dread through me. "Nakita holds his life. She chooses if he lives or dies."

Oh God, I've killed him, I thought, the panic almost paralyzing. I had to talk to Nakita.

"There is hope," Ron soothed as my thoughts spun, but there was no comfort in his touch on my shoulder. Instead, a warning lifted in me. Behind him, Barnabas fumed. "I'm going to continue to speak on your behalf," Ron said, as if Josh's probable death was sad but trifling. "What I'm most concerned about is you. Dissociating yourself from your amulet like you did should have been impossible. That you're dead probably accounted for your ability to do it. Regardless, I'm sure you damaged your amulet. Don't do it again. Some of this is my fault. I should've looked in on your progress, but Barnabas didn't tell me you were having trouble."

He didn't care about Josh. Not really. Warning was thick in me, and I pulled out from under his grip. And why was he blaming Barnabas? Barnabas said it was my amulet that prevented me from thought-touching, not my lack of skill or lack of trying— and Ron should have known that. He was hiding something.

"Grace said I cracked it," I said warily, but I wouldn't pull it from behind my shirt to show him.

Behind Ron, Barnabas stood stiff and tense. I saw a hint of the avenging angel in him as his eyes silvered. "I'm going home," he said to Ron, pain showing in his brow. "They'll let me in. They have to. I have to tell them about the black wings. They can get them out of her."

Home? I thought. As in heaven? Why *wouldn't* they let him in? He wasn't just earthbound, but barred from heaven? Just who were the bad guys here?

Fear slid through me like a knife, born of the sudden realization that everything I thought was true probably wasn't.

"Barnabas, shut up," Ron said as he rose between us, smaller than Barnabas but deathly serious. "I'll send word, and Nakita will be fine. They won't let you back, and I've got work to do. Stay with Madison. Try to keep her out of trouble. And keep your mouth shut!" His eyes were almost black, carrying a mix of anger, frustration, and . . . uncertainty. "You understand me? I can't fix this if you interfere. Keep your mouth . . . shut."

The image of Nakita arched in pain, white wings stretched high as she screamed, lifted through my memory. I had hurt one of heaven's angels. Who was Barnabas? Who had I been spending my nights with on my roof?

Scared, I watched Ron stride from the building, vanishing as he found the sun. I turned to Barnabas, shrinking back when he made a sound of anger and flopped into the chair next to me, his brow furrowed and his expression cross. He didn't move. Not one fidget or blink.

"She was trying to kill me," I said. "She was trying to kill Josh! She was going to—"

"Take you to Kairos. You said that," he said abruptly. There was a hint of fear in him. It wasn't fear of me, but fear for himself. He wasn't going to shut up as Ron had told him, and I shivered.

"So many religions, Madison," he said, "but only one resting place, and she was going to put you right back on that path that you skipped off when you claimed Kairos's amulet."

"Nakita's not from hell," I guessed, knowing my face was white. "You are."

Barnabas jerked straight. "Me? No," he said, coloring as if embarrassed. "Not hell. I don't even know if there is such a place other than what we make for ourselves. But I'm not from heaven . . . anymore. I left because I disagreed with seraph fate. They won't let me back. They won't let any of us light reapers back." Jaw tight, he exhaled, putting a hand to his head and rubbing his temples. "I should have told you, but it's embarrassing."

"But you're a light reaper!" I said, confused. "Light is good; dark is bad."

He scowled at me. "Light is for human choice, easily seen. Dark is for hidden seraph fate, no choice to glean."

"Oh! That would have been nice to know!" I shouted. "How come no one bothered to tell me that?!" I added, frustrated, scared, and a little relieved that Barnabas wasn't from hell, just kicked out of heaven. There was a difference, right?

The receptionist peeked out from a doorway, disappearing when she decided I was upset about Josh, not a little misunderstanding about light and dark.

Barnabas's thoughts were clearly somewhere else. "I don't understand what Ron is doing," he said to himself, gaze distant, and unaware that I was having a meltdown. "I believe in choice, but after what's happened, I don't know. You're a nice person, Madison, and I like you, but you put black wings in Nakita. That's . . . a terrible thing. Maybe the seraphs are right. Maybe you need to go where you belong. Maybe fate has a place in the world. Fighting it has only made things worse."

Where I belong? Does he mean like home with my dad, or like dead? I swallowed hard. I was not the one who'd been kicked out of heaven. "It was an accident."

"Was it an accident that you worked to learn how to go invisible?" he asked earnestly. "Was it an accident that you used that knowledge to break the hold Nakita's amulet had on you? Was it an accident that she fell through you? Or was it fate?" His head slowly shook back and forth, dark curls shifting. "I should've realized what Ron was doing sooner." His eyes narrowed. "I still don't believe it. I didn't want to believe it."

My mouth was dry. Just what *was* Ron doing? Barnabas knew something I didn't, and by God, I was going to find out. "Barnabas," I started, but the phone at the desk hummed and the nurse came back to answer it. She gave me an encouraging smile when she sat down, telling me that Josh was okay. Or at least not getting any worse. Distracted, I settled back in my chair, and, hearing a dry leaf crunch, I picked it out of my hair. I held it for a moment, then set it on the nearby table. Did I really want to know the truth? *Yeah. I do.*

I watched the line Barnabas's duster made against the dull carpet as I screwed my courage up, wondering if the coat was his wings in disguise. My mind shifted back to Ron dragging Barnabas away from me at the school's parking lot, and then just now, when Ron cautioned Barnabas to keep his mouth shut so he could fix things, the awful feeling of Ron's hand on me when he tried to comfort me. "Barnabas," I whispered, "what's Ron not telling me?"

Looking up, I saw his jaw clench. "It's not my place."

Fear made my heart give a thump, but then it stopped. "You want to tell me. You tried at the school parking lot, and I see you want to tell me now. If you believe in choice, tell me so I can make a good one."

His eyes lifted, falling first upon my amulet, then my eyes, and I shivered.

"Ron is hiding who you are from the seraphs so he can shift the balance between fate and choice by misleading you," he said flatly. "That's what I think he's doing."

"He said he was talking to them!" I argued, then hesitated. "Misleading me? Why?"

Eyes fixed on mine, Barnabas quietly said, "You're the new timekeeper, Madison. The dark one."

I blinked. "I am not," I said belligerently.

But instead of arguing with me, he smiled bitterly. "I told you there's a reason you can't touch my thoughts," he said, his gaze alighting on my amulet. "You've got a dark timekeeper amulet. If it were otherwise, our resonances would be close enough that we could talk, but they are on opposite ends of the spectrum. Ron knows that. Ron knows everything. He's just not saying anything."

Reaching down, I touched the black stone, then dropped it. "Maybe it doesn't work because I'm dead."

Barnabas turned away, and his chest rose and fell in a heavy sigh. "The only reason you succeeded in claiming a timekeeper's amulet is because you are one."

"No!" I exclaimed. "I was able to claim it because I was human."

He shook his head. "You could touch it because you were human, but you claimed it because of who you are. You went on to teach yourself how to dissociate yourself from it and still hold that claim. You commanded Grace, gave her a name that bound her and broke the charge that Ron put on her. You're a rising timekeeper, Madison, one of two people born to this millennium with the ability to survive the bending of time."

I stared at him, panic starting to wind its way through my spine. Me? A dark timekeeper? I didn't believe in fate. He had to be wrong. "Has Ron said so?" I whispered.

He shifted his feet in their dirty sneakers and scooted forward. Leaning over his knees, he eyed me from under his mop of curls. "No," he admitted, and I exhaled in relief. "But you are. Madison, timekeepers are mortal for a reason. The earth changes, people change, values change. To ask a human who was born in the time of the pyramids to understand someone who takes for granted that man can see the earth from space isn't reasonable, and so when change spills over itself in its rush to happen, new timekeepers take over."

He glanced at the receptionist and inched closer. "I've seen it before, like the turning of a wheel. Rising timekeepers are found and taught, learning until the amulet is passed on and the old timekeeper resumes aging, picking up where his or her life was disrupted by the divine. That you're dead complicates things, but this is who you are."

"No I'm not!" I protested. "I'm just me. And even if I was a timekeeper, I wouldn't be the dark timekeeper. I don't believe in fate. I just took Kairos's stone to stay alive!"

Frowning, Barnabas shot a look at the busy receptionist. "Taking it might have been a choice, but fate put you there to do it. If you were an innocent scything, Ron would have given you to the seraphs that first day. But he didn't." Barnabas's frown deepened. "I should have known then, but I never guessed he'd stoop so low as to keep you in the dark with lies."

"Ron said he told the seraphs about me, to ask them to let

me keep the stone," I said, bewildered. "If he didn't, why do I still have it?"

"Because Kairos hasn't told them you have it, either."

"Why?" I asked. I couldn't think. I was numb. I needed an answer, and I couldn't grasp enough to guess it for myself.

Barnabas shifted in his chair, pulling his coat around himself. "I'm guessing Kairos wants you destroyed so he doesn't have to give up his place, and if the seraphs find out you exist, even dead as you are, they will force him to abide by their will. Only if you are destroyed will they be obliged to allow him to remain the dark timekeeper through the turn of another wheel."

Kairos would live forever. Immortality—a higher court. That's why he killed me, then came after me. He wanted to destroy my soul completely. Panic started up again. "No. You're wrong. I simply have the wrong amulet," I said. "I just need to give it back. I need to return Nakita's amulet, too," I babbled as Barnabas flopped back to look at the ceiling. "Tell her I'm sorry. Maybe she'll let Josh live."

"If Nakita finds you, she'll take you to Kairos," Barnabas said to the ceiling. "Being sorry isn't going to change anything. You've already claimed the dark timekeeper amulet. You're it, Madison. For Kairos to reclaim it, your soul has to be destroyed! Only one or the other of you can be the dark timekeeper."

I felt dizzy. There had to be a way out of this. "One or the other? I don't think so," I said, my head hurting. "I can dissociate from my amulet. Maybe the reason I can is because it doesn't really belong to me. You ever think of that? If I can give it fully back to Kairos, then maybe I'm the rising light timekeeper."

Barnabas's foot quit jumping up and down, and he turned to me, considering it. "Ron said not to dissociate from your amulet."

I shivered, breathless with hope. "And Ron's been lying to me—to us. I say chance it. Barnabas, I am not the rising dark timekeeper!" Thinking, I looked away from his intent expression. "I need to talk to Kairos," I muttered. "Where does he live?"

Barnabas's jaw dropped. "You are not going to talk to Kairos!" he said. "And besides, I don't know." The fallen angel turned in his chair to face me, bringing a leg up onto the cushion. "Madison, even if you are the rising light timekeeper and you can give his amulet back to him, Kairos will destroy your soul anyway to slide the balance of things his way."

I couldn't afford to think like that. "He's mortal, so he lives on earth, right?" I asked, standing and looking at the empty reception desk. "If Kairos wants his amulet, he's going to have to give me my body," I said, flicking the amulet, heavy around my neck. "I bet Nakita knows where he lives. Is she okay? Did they get the black wings out of her? You can hear the songs between heaven and earth. What are they saying?"

Barnabas remained where he was, looking up at me from under his curly hair in disbelief. "Madison," he protested.

"Is she okay?" I said loudly, hand on my hip. "Can you call someone? Come on! What's the point of being a reaper if you don't do anything?"

His eyes narrowed at me for a moment in annoyance; then a smile quirked the corners of his lips. "She's okay," he said, and a knot eased in my middle. "But this is a bad idea."

I pulled him up, surprised that he moved so easily. "Yeah, but it's an idea. And if I'm a rising timekeeper, then I'm going to be your boss someday. Come on. Help me find Nakita."

Barnabas dug in his heels, and his hand pulled from mine as I continued on a step without him. "You're not going to be anyone's boss if you're dead," he said wryly.

"I have to apologize," I said, reaching for his hand and tugging him forward another step. "And give her her amulet back. Maybe if I do, she will let Josh live. Maybe that's why she hasn't killed him. She's waiting for me."

A frown creased his forehead. "You want to give a dark reaper an amulet. Are you even hearing yourself?"

"It's hers," I said. "What is the *problem*?"

"Ron will freak. He'll take my amulet away," Barnabas muttered as he glanced at the parking lot in worry. "I shouldn't have told you."

I put a hand on my hip, seeing every second as one more moment that Josh's life was still hanging by a thread. "You know you did right. I'm not asking you to leave me. If Ron takes your amulet away, I'll make you another. Unless this is another lie and I'm just a poor slob who got mixed up in this and I'm not a rising timekeeper." Man, was I glad the receptionist was gone.

Still he vacillated. "Why are you listening to Ron!" I exclaimed, frustrated. "He knew what I was and didn't tell me. He told you to teach me something he knew I couldn't do. Will you just help me?! I have to try to save Josh. I have to try to save myself. I can be me again!"

Barnabas's brown eyes searched mine. "You've always been you."

I backed up, not knowing what he was going to decide. "Will you help me?"

He stood beside me, his duster shifting about his ankles as his feet scuffed. "You see a choice here?"

My head bobbed up and down. "I see a chance." *And a way to get out of here before my dad or Josh's parents show up.*

Barnabas looked to the parking lot and the setting sun, grimacing. "I can't believe I'm going to do this," he said.

"You'll help me?" I said breathlessly, scared and elated all at the same time.

"I am going to get in so much trouble," he said as if to himself, and together we turned to the double doors. "I can take you to a safe spot. Nakita can't hurt you there. Though I don't think it will do any good."

"Thank you," I said as we walked through the doors purposefully, my stomach fluttering.

I would convince Nakita to give me Josh's life for a lousy hunk of rock, then do the same with Kairos for *my* life. Just watch me.

Eleven

I tensed my muscles and screwed my eyes shut when the green tops of the forest grew close. I didn't want to watch as Barnabas closed his wings about us and dove into a small opening in the canopy. My stomach dipped and fell. There was a brief rush of wind in the leaves, and the air cooled. I opened my eyes as he swooped to dodge a tree and landed with a sharp pull-up on a mossy log. It started to fall apart, and I jumped off as it crumbled with a soft hush.

My tangled hair covered my face when Barnabas pushed backward once with his wings to stop his momentum. By the time I turned, he was standing behind the log, his wings gone and his coat covering his narrow shoulders. Worry tightened his features, clear even in the gloom, and I gazed up at the canopy. The trees were big and the underbrush almost nonexistent. Soft loam cushioned my feet, and I clasped my arms around myself, feeling the damp. Mounds dotted the space with no pattern I could see. They looked like . . . graves.

"Where are we?" I said as I took an awkward step over the log to be closer to Barnabas.

"A spot of ground," he said softly. "The earth would shake to feel the touch of a seraph, but there are a few places where the ground is strong enough, and in the past, immortals have used them to conduct business on earth. The circles across the sea have huge stones marking them, but here, where people lived harmoniously with nature until driven out, they're marked with mounds that shelter bribes to the angels to leave them and their children in peace." He turned to me, and I shivered at his suddenly alien look. "It's a neutral place. If blood is spilled here, a seraph will come. Nakita won't want that."

I scanned the open wood, feeling my skin prickle. "It feels funny."

"It does, doesn't it?"

There was nothing to hear but the wind in the highest leaves. "How do I tell Nakita I want to talk?"

Barnabas silently stepped from me, moving a good twenty feet away so that his amulet signature wouldn't mix with mine. Eyes on the darkening trees, he said, "I imagine she's looking for you. You'd better be sure of this."

"I am," I said confidently, but inside I was worried. I was exposed, my soul singing to those who could hear it, chiming like a bell, making a spot of light that Nakita could follow. My jaw clenched when a black wing flew silently across the space between the ground and the trees, but then I decided it was really a crow. I looked up, my attention drawn by something unseen.

Barnabas shifted his feet, and a twig snapped. "I feel it too," he whispered.

I swallowed hard. "What is it?"

His eyes slowly moved back and forth. "I don't know. It feels like a reaper, but afraid. Like a human."

Barnabas's gaze darted behind me. "Madison! Drop!" he shouted, and I fell into a sloppy front fall, getting a faceful of earthy loam. The weight of a stone rolled across my back, and then was gone. I looked up, spitting my hair and dirt out of my mouth.

With wings so white they glowed in the dusk, Nakita came to earth, spinning so her feet barely touched the ground before her wings vanished like a memory.

"You're okay!" I shouted, thinking it was one of the stupidest things I'd ever said.

"The seraphs lie to me as well," the reaper snarled, fear and anger twisting her once beautiful features. I had no idea what she was talking about, and I stared blankly at her.

"Nakita, wait!" Barnabas shouted as he lunged to get between us. The light reaper darted back when a gleam of steel slashed down. Nakita's arms were extended and her back bowed as she struck again. I gasped as I reached out in a useless warning, but Barnabas's own blade met her sword, pulled from forever and nothing, and I shivered as the sound seemed to echo and made the trees tremble. Kairos must have given her a new amulet. She didn't need the one I wanted to return to her. Her sword had a black stone now, and the jewel on Barnabas's blade had shifted farther down the spectrum, blazing a glorious yellow. Nakita's looked dead, a flat black.

"Madison wants to parlay," Barnabas said as he held Nakita's weapon unmoving against his own. "Sheathe your blade in this holy spot."

Nakita smiled, the determination on her face frightening. She looked nothing like herself, dressed in white garb that was twin to Ron's robes. "I need her," she said, her voice musical as it rose and fell. "You brought her. She's mine."

Barnabas took a step back, and the humming in my ears ceased when their blades no longer touched. "She brought herself. She wants to apologize. To not listen would shame you."

With a flourish, Nakita stepped back, wild and extravagant as she gestured for me to speak. I didn't think she cared what I might say, but it was my only shot.

Scared, I faced her with Barnabas at my elbow. "Nakita, I'm sorry," I said, my words vanishing into the gloom of dusk. "I didn't know the black wings would stay in you. I was only trying to stop you from killing Josh. I brought your amulet back," I said, hand trembling as I extended it. "It's not a bribe, but please let Josh live."

Her face twisted in a frown, but she caught the amulet when I tossed it to her, shoving it into her belt. "Kairos gives me my amulet, not you," she said. "And I need your pity less than I need your apology. The seraphs say I am perfectly fine. I am perfect!" she screamed to the sky, then turned to me, panting and eyes wild. "But they lie."

Barnabas pulled me back a step. "We need to leave. She's broken. This isn't going to accomplish anything."

"I'm broken, too," I said, thinking of my interrupted life, and I jerked out of his grip. "Nakita, will you take a message to Kairos for me? He has my body. I want it back. I'll give him his amulet for it if he promises to leave me alone. I just want to be the way I was. Please. I'm tired of being afraid."

At the word *afraid*, she trembled, and a shimmer of air behind her shifted to show her wings arching over her, larger than seemed possible, the tips of the longest feathers shaking. They may have gotten the black wings out of her, but they left within her something a reaper was never created to understand. Fear. And it had come from me. My memories.

"I'm not your messenger angel," she said bitterly. "But we *are* going to Kairos. You're a thief. A liar. With your body and soul and my scythe, he can make me as I was. As everything was. He promised!"

Kairos still has my body. Thank you, God.

"You aren't taking her," Barnabas said, clueless that Nakita was now a hundred times more dangerous. She had the power of angels cleaved to the will of humanity. Fear and a knowledge of death had made her so. *I* had made her so.

"She's mine as she stands there." Dropping into a hunched position, Nakita dragged her new sword forward, the tip cutting into the ground to make the moss split like a wound.

I shook my head, backing up. "Nakita, listen to me. I just want my body back, alive and unharmed. He doesn't have to destroy my soul for the amulet. I can dissociate from it."

She straightened as a laugh, cruel and horrible to hear, burst from her. Barnabas shifted closer to me in support. "Kairos needs you dead to make me whole again," she said. "Barnabas, get out of my way, or you'll go down first."

"You wouldn't." Barnabas pushed me behind him as Nakita pulled her sword from the earth and casually wiped the dirt from it upon her leg. "A seraph will come. You won't risk it."

"Why not?!" Nakita shouted, then fell back a step, wide-eyed. "I have nothing, Barnabas!" she screamed. "Do you know what it is like to fear? I will *laugh* if a seraph should slay me for violating one of their places on earth. It would at least be over and I wouldn't have to be afraid anymore!"

Barnabas didn't understand, and his brow furrowed. "Afraid?"

An ugly noise came from Nakita, low, almost a growl. It sifted through my brain and paralyzed me. And then she moved.

I stifled a shriek as she lunged at Barnabas, white wings

unfurling behind her. Barnabas dropped to a knee, his own gray wings wide as he darted back, airborne. I retreated, scrambling for cover. A great wind churned the leaves from the forest floor. A clang of steel hurt my ears. They were locked, arms straining, Barnabas standing, his wings beating to find the force to push Nakita back.

"I *will* have *her*!" Nakita screamed as her wings beat wildly, and she tried to press Barnabas into the ground with her will alone. "I will not be this way! I cannot!"

Barnabas kicked out to shove her off. Gray and white wings struck the trees. Silver flashed in the gloom as Barnabas dove forward, his disadvantage clear. He didn't want to spill blood. Nakita didn't care, and she struck wildly at Barnabas, the light reaper countering each blow more slowly than the last. The dark reaper was fighting with a savage desperation that only humans possess, and it was starting to tell upon Barnabas.

A heavy feeling about my neck shocked me, and I grasped my amulet, feeling as if the earth had vanished under my feet. Someone . . . someone was trying to use it! And when Nakita screamed, I knew it was her attempting to duplicate what I'd done to go invisible. She was too far away for my amulet to hold her solid, but Barnabas's wasn't.

With a wild scream, Nakita smashed her sword into Barnabas's blade, knocking it from him. The amulet about his neck flared and went still. He was helpless. Mouth open in a howl, Nakita jumped right at him. Barnabas braced for an impact that never came as Nakita broke her connection to her amulet and went invisible, diving through him as if he were water.

"Barnabas, look out!" I shouted, but it was too late. Nakita appeared behind the light reaper, spinning to put her sword against his neck. Her arms braced to pull.

"Nakita, no!" I shrieked, scrambling to stand before them. The dark reaper hesitated, her lips pulled back in a savage, victorious smile. They were posed, two angels of death locked together, one wild and crazed, the other beaten and shocked.

"W-where did you learn that?" Barnabas stammered, frozen at the feel of another reaper's blade against his throat.

Nakita's eyes never left mine as she leaned forward, whispering in Barnabas's ear, "It's amazing what you can do once you know nothing lasts forever unless you make it so."

My mouth was dry. "Don't kill him," I pleaded. "Please, Nakita."

"Silly girl," Nakita said, her lips twisted into an ugly expression. "Why do you care? No one else does. He failed to protect you, brought you to me. And now, you're going to die."

"I'll go with you! Just don't kill him. Take me to Kairos," I demanded, shaking. "Let me talk to him."

"That's exactly what I intend to do," Nakita said, and then she moved, drawing back.

"Nakita, don't!" I screamed as she brought the butt of her sword against Barnabas's skull. Silently the light reaper's gray wings drooped and he fell forward, slumped against the mossy earth. His wings covered him, and he looked asleep, an angel resting on a forest floor.

My heart was beating again, and I started to back up. Nakita shook her wings and smiled. One soft feather slipped from her, the pure white drifting to land on the green, green moss.

I ran.

There was a whoosh of air, and she had me. That fast, and it was over. "Let me go!" I cried. I knew going invisible wouldn't help if she could, too. "Why can't you leave me alone?!"

"I want myself back," Nakita snarled as she held me tight against her. "I don't want to be afraid anymore. The black wings," she said, her words clipped as her voice rose in pitch. "I've never known fear. I've seen it, thought you were all weak for it, but you aren't. I don't want to be afraid anymore. I want to be the way I was. Kairos can make me the way I was. But he needs his amulet to do it."

My amulet, I thought defiantly, then shrieked as we were abruptly airborne, ducking when we exploded through the canopy and back into the light. Her arm was tight around me, and my legs flailed until my heels found her feet and I stood upon them. It was a show of cooperation, but at least my guts weren't being shoved up into my lungs.

"Nakita, I'm sorry," I said as we ascended. "I didn't know the black wings would hurt you. You were trying to kill me!"

"It was my task, your fate," she said, gripping me tightly. "I can't exist the way I am now. I will be the way I was!"

The air was cold. Without warning, Nakita swooped into a dive, her wings folding around us, cocooning us in pillow-soft warmth. I fought her as my stomach dropped and vertigo told me we were falling.

"Be still," Nakita snarled, and then the world turned inside out.

I screamed, my mind unable to take the absolute absence of everything. No sound, no touch, nothing. It was as if I were a black wing, never having existed but having the terror of knowing there was more and it was now lost to me. I was falling, and there was nothing within my experience to tell me it would ever end.

Suddenly Nakita's wings were about me once more, infusing their warmth into me. I breathed her scent in, gasping in relief, feeling her presence bring me back to sanity. We weren't moving, and when her arm about me fell away, my knees hit a hard floor. Struggling to rise with my shaking muscles, I scrambled backward, getting to my feet and trying to figure out what had happened. My back hit a thick pillar holding up a white canopy, and I froze, mouth gaping.

I was outside, standing on a veranda of black marble shot through with gold veins. There was no railing between it and the drop-off leading to a narrow beach down below. The sun was just above the horizon, but the cool, damp feel in the air was wrong for sunset. It was *rising* over a flat ocean, not setting, and as I looked at the sparse vegetation with its small leaves and tough skin designed to survive drought, I realized I was somewhere on the other side of the earth.

A scuffing noise jerked my attention around. It was Nakita, but she was ignoring me as I pulled out of my instinctive crouch. Her wings were gone, and she placidly stood beside Kairos, who was sitting behind a small table covered with old books and a breakfast tray. The dark timekeeper was dressed in loose robes like Ron usually wore, looking young, fabulously refined and elegant, poised and tall, his calm expression holding a satisfied expectancy.

Scared, I glanced behind me to a low building built into the hillside, its wide windows open to the elements. Curtains shifted in and out of the house, moving in the breeze. I could die here, and my dad would never know. "This is your house, isn't it?" I whispered, and the wind carried my words to Kairos.

He smiled as he stood and came forward.

I was dead. I was so-o-o-o dead.

Twelve

"Perceptive," Kairos said, his voice as hard as his expression.

My yellow sneakers squeaked as I turned to run, but there was nowhere to go. In a blur of motion, Nakita was beside me, and I lurched to stay out of her reach. Grimacing, she shoved me, and I fell. My elbow hit the black granite, jarring me all the way to my spine. I tried to stand, falling again when Nakita hooked a foot under me and rolled me onto my back.

I froze as they both stood over me, the scent of dirt rising from a smear on Nakita's leg. The black stone at my back was cool with the chill of night, and the sky held a delicate, transparent light.

"How quickly the fate of angels can fail," Kairos said, his words rising and falling like music. I'd once thought I could hear the sea in his voice—that he had been beautiful, embodying elegance, refinement, sophistication—but all that was left was the reek of dead salt water, stinking and putrid. My eyes flicked to the scythe in his hand, and I recognized it as the one he had killed me with at the bottom of the embankment.

"Not again!" I babbled, lurching to fling myself away. My back found a pillar, and I slid my back up it to stand with my fingers clenching the raised ridges. Gasping in reflex, I ducked as Nakita swung her blade at me.

A sharp *crack* echoed through the air, and I looked up to see that Kairos had brought his own blade to bear, holding back a deathblow with a frightening ease.

"Patience, Nakita," the dark timekeeper said. "You can kill her, but not until I retrieve her body. All three have to come together at once; otherwise nothing changes. I simply need a moment to find it."

I darted away, trying to put space between us. Nakita's gaze flicked to me. "You told me it was close."

"It is. Will you give me a moment to concentrate? Once I find it, it will be here, and you can kill her."

He sounded bothered, and I stood, terrified, at a loss as to what to do. Sure, I'd gotten away, but I wasn't going anywhere. I was on an island. I knew the feeling of the earth when water pounded on all sides. "Kairos, give me back my body and let me go, and I'll give you your stupid amulet," I said as I scanned the open horizon for an escape, but I was shaking, and I cursed my voice when it quavered. "I don't care if I'm a rising timekeeper.

All I want is to be left alone, okay?"

Kairos laughed, throwing his head back and letting the long sound roll out, and I realized that Nakita had blinked at my words. She hadn't known. Kairos hadn't told her. I had been a mistake to her, nothing more. "Who told you?" Kairos asked, wiping an eye. "Not Ron. Or did you figure it out? Amazing. I fully intend to give you your body back, because until you're dead and gone, your giving me my amulet won't allow me to use it."

"I can dissociate from it," I said. "I learned how yesterday. It will be all yours. Ron can make me a new one. Just give me my body and let me go, okay?"

The air shifted, and I spun. "Ron!" I shouted as I saw him. *Barnabas. Is he okay?* Then my eyes narrowed. Why was I glad to see Ron?

Nakita swooped forward to grab my arm, and I fought her—until I found her blade at my throat, the thumb-sized, dead-looking jewel glinting dully inches from my eye. *Damn it! How did she move that fast?* Kairos's claim that my body was nearby froze my muscles. If he produced it, she could kill me for good.

"Too late, Ron," Kairos said, laughing softly at my surprise. "That's funny," he said lightly to Nakita. "A master of time running late."

My feet slipped on the smooth stone. If not for Nakita catching me, I would have cut myself on her blade. I was so scared.

Ron bowed his head. The new sun shone on him, lighting the determination in his eyes when he brought his gaze back to me. Determination and . . . guilt? It was about freaking time.

"Let her go, Nakita," he said persuasively. "Kairos can't help you, even if he gets his amulet back. Madison is a rising keeper. It's already fated whose place she's going to take."

Her breath came in softly, and as her grip on me loosened, I could feel her confusion. Kairos strode forward, saying, "I didn't lie. I won't know for sure I can't do it until I try."

"She is a rising timekeeper?" Nakita questioned, and I started when her sword smoothly moved, shifting from my neck to point at him. Seeing it, Kairos halted with a comical swiftness. She was still holding me, though, her arm around my neck. Shock showed on his refined features, which he quickly hid.

"Nakita," he coaxed, "I might be able to help you. Put your blade away."

"You told me you could pluck the fear from me," Nakita said, holding me tighter. "You told me the seraphs sang that she was fated to die, and to take her. Is she a rising timekeeper? Did you send me to scythe a timekeeper because you fear death? Chronos believes it!"

Nakita's voice thundered in my ear, the righteous anger of an angel wronged. The hem of Kairos's robe trembled as he took three steps back, his jaw clenched. The moment seemed to hesitate, and I wondered if I was being held for my death . . . or my protection.

"So I lied," Kairos admitted, returning to his table and turning sideways to finger the small pitcher on the tray. His shadow from the rising sun stretched long to touch my feet, and I shivered as the light glinted on his less powerful amulet. "I have ruled both you and time for more than a thousand years, Nakita. I'm not going to go quietly because the seraphs *fated* it was time for me to step down, teach another, and fade into death. And not for a girl hardly old enough to be counted a woman."

"She's as old as you were when you murdered your predecessor," Ron said sourly. "Funny how these things work out."

Kairos's upper lip trembled, but his eyes were fixed on Nakita's. "She can't be a timekeeper," he said tightly. "She's dead. I killed her myself."

Ron moved a step closer, halting when Nakita's sword shifted to him for a moment, then back to Kairos. "She stole your amulet," he said. "I don't think it matters what her state of aliveness is if she managed that. Madison has already claimed her birthright. She wrested the control of a guardian angel from me by simply naming her, and she now stands in Nakita's protection. It's too late. You've lost, Kairos. It's over. Let her go. Accept it."

And yet, I was still in a dark reaper's grip.

"Kairos?" Nakita asked, her voice high as she struggled to piece it together. I was right there with her, and a wave of vertigo made my knees watery. Frightened, I stiffened as the soft wind shifted my hair into my eyes, momentarily blocking Kairos from my sight with Nakita's sword unmoving between us.

"I'm not the rising dark timekeeper," I said as Nakita pulled me back a step. "I'm the rising light. That's why I want to trade Kairos his amulet for my body. Ron, he's got my body. I can go back to the way I was! Tell him I can break my hold on his amulet." My gaze darted to Kairos, seeing his disbelief. "I can! I've done it before! Ron, tell him! Tell him I'm the rising light timekeeper!"

But Ron was looking at the ground, scaring me.

With a false ease, Kairos poured amber liquid into a crystal cup, sipping it lightly before setting it down. "Still don't have it all?" he said. "You were fated to be my student, Madison; why else would I scythe you? Ron can't take you now even if he wanted to. He's been teaching the rising light timekeeper for over a year."

What the . . . My frantic gaze went to Ron, reading in his downcast expression that Kairos was telling the truth. "You son of a dead puppy," I whispered. "You knew? You're teaching someone else? Is that why you passed me off to Barnabas?"

Ron winced. He came forward a step, and Nakita pulled me back two. Disgusted, I shook Nakita's hold off me and stood upright in the new day under my own power. The dark reaper faced the sun and knelt with her sword upon one knee and her head bowed—she looked like she was praying, hair hiding her face as a soft, eerie keening came from her.

"I did it for mankind, Madison," Ron said persuasively. "You could stop the wrongful deaths if I could get you to align your-self with me. Think of it! A dark timekeeper who believed in choice? There'd be no more scythes, no more lives cut short. Kairos would be bereft of power, leaving only peace behind as you took his place."

"Why would she align herself with you?!" Kairos exclaimed. "You hid her from the seraphs behind allegations and investiga-tions, denied her existence from those who would have righted things. It was your own actions that forced the truth of her existence from where we'd both hidden it so we could fight over her like dogs over scraps. You whispered false truths into her ear until her choices were the ones you wanted. You passed her instruction off to *a reaper*, giving him a task you knew he couldn't manage while you tutored the one fated to replace you, intending to leave Madison bereft of skills in case the truth should come out and she took my place, safely ignorant and at a disadvantage." Kairos turned to me, disgust in his eyes. "And you let him."

My head moved back and forth in denial. I hadn't known. How could I?

I jumped when Nakita was suddenly at my side, the gentle touch of her wings brushing me. Her sword was gone, and I stared at her, seeing her confusion, knowing what she was feel-ing, since I was feeling it myself: betrayal, dismay, fear.

"At least I didn't try to kill her," Ron muttered.

"No, you kept her ignorant."

"I'm the one who saved her!" Ron shouted back.

"You didn't save me," I said, lips barely moving. "I died. Remember?"

The light breeze coming up from the beach lifted my hair to make the purple tips tickle my cheek. I tried to understand. It didn't make sense. I could not be the rising dark timekeeper. I didn't believe in fate.

Ron started forward, and I jerked out of my fog. "Stop!" I shouted, gripping my amulet with my other hand outstretched, and he halted, stymied.

"The seraphs fated Madison to take your place?" Nakita said, her voice cracking. "You sent me to kill the one who would be my master? The next who would uphold seraph will?"

Kairos frowned at her. "She wouldn't be your new master if you would let me destroy her soul. With her gone, I will live forever, able to claim a place at a higher court." Kairos pulled himself into a proud stance. "I will be immortal. Immortal, Nakita!" he said, his expression becoming fervent as he gestured, almost knocking over his cup. "It would be enough to shift the tides of time to our favor forever. Imagine it!"

"You promised to help me," Nakita whispered, her voice softer than the wind.

Kairos glanced at her in annoyance, but his eyes narrowed as he realized the threat she was. "Give me your amulet," he said, holding out his hand, and when she didn't, he strode forward, anger and dominance in his movement.

I stifled a gasp when Nakita shoved me behind her, and my feet scrambled to keep me upright. There was a sharp *ping* that seemed to make the new sunlight shiver, and when I looked, Nakita's amulet was in Kairos's hand and he was striding to the nearby table. He had made her helpless. *Crap. Now what?*

"I'm still your master, you ignorant angel," he said as Nakita's source of power clinked upon the table; then his smile chilled me to the bone. "Now. Madison. About your body."

Oh, God. He had my body. He could destroy my soul. Ron stood unmoving, not that I expected anything from him.

Nakita dropped to a knee before Kairos, her face pale and a ribbon of moisture slipping from her eye. "You said you could make me well," she said, grief clear in her tone. "I don't want to be afraid."

Despite my own fear, pity rose through me. She was fallen, an angel doubly betrayed. The innocence of a wild thing of power given knowledge of death.

"You promised, Kairos," Nakita said softly as tears slipped from her and she wiped them away, shock showing briefly at their presence. "I suffered black wings eating my memory. Memory is all I have. I believed you. You sent me to kill her because you fear death?"

"I will be immortal!" Kairos shouted, his anger bursting forth. "How can you presume to know what it's like to fear death? You've existed since time began and will until it ends!"

Nakita stood, the air shimmering where her wings would

be. "I know now what it's like to fear death, but I still live by seraph will," she said, her voice shaking. "I live by it, and you will die by it."

Kairos smirked, fingering her amulet on the table. "How, Nakita? You belong to me."

But then she pulled from her belt a white rock, bound by black wire and laced on a simple black cord. It didn't look like the amulet I had returned to her in the woods, and Kairos shook his head as if it meant nothing—until she rubbed a thumb across it and what looked like salt fell away to show a simple black stone glowing with infinity. It *was* the stone I'd returned to her in the woods. As if I had been her keeper. I'd stained it with my tears—gifting her with a symbol of my grief and an atonement for having broken the purity of her existence.

Nakita's hand fisted about it. "I accept you," she said to me, though her frightening grimace was for Kairos.

"No!" I shrieked, reaching out when the glint of her sword flashed a pure black. Nakita leaped forward to send her blade cleanly through Kairos.

Ron took several steps forward, crying out in dismay, but it was too late. It was done.

Kairos looked at his unmarked middle, blinking when he brought his gaze up, fixing first on the violet stone, then her eyes. "You've failed us," he whispered, and then he collapsed.

Nakita reached out and caught him gently, almost lovingly, as she eased the dark timekeeper to the polished floor. "Fate,

Kairos," Nakita whispered, crying as her hands slid from him, and she closed his eyes so they wouldn't look to the heavens. "The seraphs fated her taking your place. Your span was done. There is no failure. There is only change."

"Oh my God!" I shouted, terrified as I stood there. "You killed him! How could you . . . ? He's dead!"

Ron made a sound of regret, and I spun to him, frightened. If Kairos was dead, then that meant— "He's not dead," I babbled. "Tell me he's not dead."

"He's gone," Ron said, and I danced back when Nakita was suddenly before me, kneeling and offering me her sword.

"Nakita, no!" I cried out, panicked.

"My lady," she insisted, pain in her fragile expression. "I am flawed."

"Stop. Stop!" I said, frantic as I tried to get her to rise. She was so beautiful. She was an angel. She shouldn't be kneeling before me. "D-don't do this," I stammered. "I'm not the dark timekeeper." I looked at Ron, standing with his hands clasped before him.

"You are the keeper of unseen justice," Nakita said, smiling at me, "sanctioned by seraphs. Able to track time and bend it to your will."

"No I'm not!" I insisted, glancing at Kairos's body. *Nakita had just killed him!*

Ron sighed heavily enough for me to hear. "Yes, you are."

My gaze went to him, and I stiffened. A figure was behind

him, hard to see against the rising sun. Ron saw where my attention was and turned. A strangled sound escaped him, and he scrambled out from between us. It was a seraph. It had to be.

"Blood has been spilled in the home of a timekeeper," the seraph said, its voice both musical and painful. It carried the power of the tides and the gentle caress of the waves upon the beach, and I almost cried to hear it. I couldn't bear it. It was too much.

"A sacrifice so you will hear my plea." Nakita stood before the seraph with her head bowed, but her sword was still at my feet, and I picked it up.

The seraph nodded, and I wondered if I should bow or curtsy or kneel or something. *Oh, God.* It was a freaking seraph, and here I was in yellow tights and skull earrings.

"She has taken her place," Nakita said. "I present her to you and ask a boon. I want to be as I was. I'm damaged." She looked up, tears marring her beautiful face. "I fear, seraph."

"That is not damage, Nakita," the seraph said gently. "That is a gift. Rejoice in your fear."

The seraph turned to me, and my mouth went dry. "I'm not the dark timekeeper," I babbled, shoving Nakita's sword back at her until she took it. "I can't be! I don't know anything!"

"You will. In time," the seraph said, wry amusement in its voice. "Until then, I will keep everything running smoothly. Don't be long. My voice is already missed from the chorus."

"But I don't believe in fate!" I exclaimed. My gaze shot to

Ron; I was thinking I was having doubts about choice, too.

"To believe in fate is not a requirement," the musical voice said, the seraph seeming to take up the entire world, though it wasn't much bigger than I was. "Kairos didn't. Apparently." I took a quick breath when it looked away from me and fixed on Ron. "You do, though. For all that you say otherwise."

Ron didn't move until the seraph looked away; then he sagged in relief.

"But I don't want the job!" I said, frantic that what I wanted didn't seem to matter. "Please, can't I just have my body and go back to the way things were?"

The seraph blinked, looking shocked—if such an emotion could be applied to the divine. "You don't want this?" it asked, and Ron took a step forward as if to protest.

"No!" I said, hope filling me. "I just want to be me." In a rush, I pulled the stone from around my neck. Gathering my courage, I darted forward, pushing the amulet into the seraph's hands. My heart was pounding again, and, embarrassed that I couldn't control it, I backed up, wondering if I'd broken a rule by getting that close. I couldn't look up at its face. It hurt.

The seraph looked at the amulet in its luminescent fingers as if holding a great treasure. The stone was blazing an infinite black, the silver wires now a hot gold. "You already are you."

"Please," I begged, darting a glance at Kairos, dead on the tiles and forgotten. "Can you just make me as I was? Put me back in my body?"

Hope buoyed me up when the seraph smiled so brightly that I squinted. "If you choose so," it said, an unexpected humor in its voice. "Where is it?"

My ecstatic shout died in dismay. "Kairos had it," I said, feeling ill when my gaze landed on Nakita, then Ron, quiet in the background. He was no help, and I turned to the seraph.

"It's got to be in the house," I said, turning to it and feeling naked without the amulet around my neck.

"It would have rotted by now," said Ron.

Horror lifted through me, and then fear. Had Kairos let my body rot? Had all of this been for nothing?

"He's right," the seraph said. "Your corporeal self is not here on earth."

I staggered to the table, sitting down heavily, my legs unable to hold me upright anymore. My elbows went onto the tiled table, and I knocked Kairos's cup over. Scrambling, I righted it, wondering why. *No one is going to drink it. It's a dead man's drink.*

"He said it was close," I whispered, numb. Where was my body if it wasn't on earth?

The sun was eclipsed, and I looked up to see the seraph sit before me, a situation both shocking and mind-numbing. "Your body is most certainly somewhere between now and the next."

My heart felt like ash, and I blinked, trying to see the angel's features. But there had been hope in its words. "Between now and the next? What does that mean?" *I'm sitting at a table with an angel on the other side of the world. How freaky is that?*

"It means that your body is lost, but the lost can be found," the seraph said. "Kairos would have put your body in the only place it would remain hidden yet be immediately accessible. Between now and the next."

Licking my lips, I snuck a glance at Kairos's dead body. "Can you take me there?"

Again, the seraph smiled, and I had to drop my gaze. "There is no *there* to go to. It just is. Within time, you'll be able to see between the now and the next." Clearing its throat in a very human gesture, the seraph extended my amulet back to me. "Do you choose to take this or will you choose to perish utterly?"

Like I really have a choice?

The wind off the ocean shifted my bangs, and I glanced at Nakita, looking lost and beautiful as she rubbed the slickness of her tears between her fingers, trying to figure them out. "Can I sort of accept it?" I asked. "Just until I find my body?"

The seraph laughed. The beautiful sound shook the air, and the table between us cracked. "And you do not believe in fate!" it said merrily, reminding me of Grace somehow.

"I'm serious," I said roughly, trying to cover up my shock at the broken table. "Can I do this until I find my body, then give the amulet back?" To be alive again was all I wanted.

Nakita had come forward, purpose replacing her confusion. Seeing her, the angel shifted its expression to one of calculation.

"If that is what you choose," it said slyly.

"Choice?" I asked sourly. "I thought you were all about fate."

"There is always choice," the seraph said.

I glanced at Kairos and stifled a shudder. "Kairos said there's only fate."

"And Chronos said there is only free will," it said with a devious lilt to its voice.

The seraph was up to something. Talking to it was very odd. Its emotions were as easy to read as a child's, but powerful beyond belief. Licking my lips, I turned so I couldn't see Kairos. "Which is right? Choice or fate?"

"They both are," it said. With a hush of sliding fabric that sounded like sunshine, the seraph knelt before me, the amulet held out in supplication.

I bolted to my feet, scared. "Don't do that," I whispered, wanting everyone to just ignore me. *I'm going to get sick. I'm going to get sick right here on this beautiful floor.*

The seraph looked up, and pain sliced through my head as our eyes met, almost blinding me. "I honor you. You can do something I cannot," it said softly. "For all I am and all I have been, you are human. You are loved for your inventiveness, both good and bad. I can kill, but you can create. You can even create . . . an end," it said wistfully. "That's something I will never be able to do. Accept this. Create."

I stared at my amulet. It was beautiful, the black stone glinting with tiny silver lights at its center like stars. I couldn't look at the seraph's face, it hurt so much, but I felt like it was smiling at me. "Madison, fate—not choice—sent Kairos to kill you. Fate gave you courage to claim his amulet. Fate caused Chronos to hide you from us. It has been fate that angled a hundred moments to bring you here. And yet, you have to choose to accept your place or return as you were."

Still I hesitated from going back. "Which would you choose?" I asked. "If you could."

The seraph laughed. "Neither, I am me. Choice? Fate? They are the same. I cannot see the difference. It is why only a human can twist time to his or her will. When you fly high enough, seeing around the corners of time is not a problem, but it makes separating the future and the past difficult."

It was a choice that wasn't one. Fate that was set by free will. I didn't want to die, so there was only one option, and as if in a dream, I reached out to take my amulet, my life. The seraph's skin was cool, and when our fingers touched, I felt the vastness of space spread before me in my thoughts. The stone was warm, and my fingers closed about it, claiming it anew.

In a graceful movement, the seraph stood. "It is done. She has taken her place."

That fast, it was done. No fanfare, no trumpets. The amulet rested in my hand, feeling like it always had. Shocked, I looked up from it. *That's it? I'm the dark timekeeper?*

Ron sighed. Nakita was at my elbow, her fear that I would cast her aside clear in her wide eyes. "What would you have me do?" she whispered, begging me to give her a task.

I looked at the seraph, confused, and it said, "You have a desire. She will see to it."

"Save Josh," I said, wonder-struck that it was that easy. After all that I had done, I only had to ask? "Help Barnabas."

Nakita's eyebrows rose and her lips parted. "I've never done that," she said, and Ron made a choking sound.

"Please," I added, curling my fingers around hers as she held her sword.

Nakita nodded. Her wings blurred into existence. The whiteness of them shimmered as she wrapped them around herself, and with a soft sigh of air, she vanished.

"It's a good beginning," the seraph said, jerking my attention back to it. "You see well, Madison. Your friend Josh isn't done doing for others yet." Smiling, it leaned close. I couldn't move as the scent of clean water flowed into me, cooling my anxiety and filling me with peace. "You should go before your father calls for you," it said, and when it kissed my forehead, I passed out.

Thirteen

It was noisy, the sound of first-day excitement punctuated by the occasional slamming locker. The teachers weren't even trying to keep a lid on it. Three Rivers was a small community, and they didn't have to stand in the hallway between classes like they did at my old school, which was too crowded to let the student body go without supervision. Yet another advantage to small-town life.

I shoved my books into my locker and pulled out my class schedule. It said *senior* across the top, and I couldn't help my smile. Senior. That was a good feeling. Even better, I wasn't the new girl anymore. Nope. I'd been ousted from that stellar position.

"What does domestic economic studies entail?" Nakita asked slowly as she squinted at the thin yellow paper in her grip. I'd helped her pick out her wardrobe this morning, and she looked good in her designer jeans and sandals that showed off her black toenails. I hadn't had to paint them that color. Apparently dark reapers had black toenails.

From my other side, Barnabas shifted his backpack higher up on his shoulder, looking like any kid in any school in his jeans and T-shirt. "You'll love it, Nakita," he said, smirking. "It will help teach you how to blend in. Try not to scythe your partner if the cookies get burned."

I stifled my laugh, trying to imagine the petite, attractive, but sometimes totally clueless dark reaper balancing a check-book or learning how to use a microwave. My gaze returned to my schedule. Physics. Study hall. Advanced English with Josh. Photography. It was going to be a good year.

Nakita stood back from the lockers as she puzzled it through, almost getting in the way of the foot traffic. "What do cook-ies have to do with economics?" she asked as she tossed her hair back in an unconscious gesture most models spend years perfecting. With that hair and those eyes, she was gorgeous, and I could already feel the stares as everyone wondered what she was doing standing next to me. The story was that she and Barnabas were exchange students, and with a little angel inter-vention, they had the background to prove it. As far as anyone knew, they were staying at my house. The truth was more . . . interesting.

Amy's voice lifted high over the surrounding babble, and I

stiffened, opening my locker and pretty much hiding behind the door. I wasn't afraid of her, but the prom queen mentality irritated the heck out of me.

"Hi!" came her cheery voice, and I cringed, since she had to be talking to Nakita. Her bevy of conformist boobs were behind her, and I pretended to be looking for something. "I'm Amy," she practically bubbled. "You must be the new girl. Is that your brother? He's kinda hot."

Barnabas stiffened to look charmingly innocent with his mop of curls and wide eyes, and I smiled. He really had no clue how good he looked.

"That dung flop?" Nakita said, her dislike almost visibly dripping into nasty puddles at Amy's designer flats. "Yes, I guess. That doesn't mean I have to like him."

"I know what you mean." Amy faked a heartfelt sigh. "I have a brother too." The girls behind her giggled when she pushed past me to Barnabas. "I'm Amy," she said, smiling as she extended her hand.

"Barnabas," the reaper said as he darted past me to give Nakita a sideways hug to avoid having to shake Amy's hand. "This is Nakita. She's my favorite sister. We're from Norway."

Norway? I couldn't help my smirk when Amy's friends started buzzing behind her.

"I thought you had an accent," Amy said, only mildly flustered at the slight dis. "Why don't you sit at my table for lunch? Both of you. You don't want to eat with dweebs."

Unable to take it anymore, I slammed my locker shut.

"Madison! Sweetie! I didn't see you there," Amy cooed. "That top is to die for," she said, gesturing. "It's so you. My little sister gave one just like that to Goodwill last year."

Nakita had been teaching me how to use my amulet to draw energy from the time stream to make a blade, and it took all I had not to practice it now. "Hi, Amy. How's the nose? Are you going to get that lump shaved off before picture day?" *That felt almost as good, though.*

Amy flushed, but I was spared her comeback when her posse parted with giggles, and Len strutted up.

In a fast motion, Nakita grabbed him by the neck and slammed him against the locker. Shocked, I stood with my mouth hanging open. Around us came oohs and catcalls. "Touch me there again, and you will die, swine," she said, every word succinct.

Len's eyes were wide, and his face was red as Nakita pressed it into the ribbed metal. Barnabas was laughing, but I didn't want to spend my first day of school in the principal's office. "Uh, Nakita?" I offered.

The reaper took a startled breath, glanced at the faces watching, and let him go. Len stumbled to catch his balance, but nothing could help him find his pride. I mean, Nakita was smaller than him, and she looked like a ditz, with her perpetual confusion. Of course, she looked like an embarrassed ditz right now.

"You're freaking whacked!" Len shouted, backing away as he fixed his shirt. "You hear me? You're Madison's friends, aren't you? You're just as whacked as her!"

I made an innocent face, trying not to laugh. Barnabas, though, was snickering—as was the entire male student body who'd seen the incident.

Amy grabbed his arm as if she was stopping him from coming after us, and she pulled him away when a teacher came around the corner. There was nothing to see, though, but excitement and laughter lingered. The guys left with loud comebacks, and the handful of estrogen trailed behind them. I exhaled, not even having realized I'd taken a breath.

"Nakita?" I said as I opened my locker again. "We need to work on your people skills."

"He touched me," she said, scowling. "He's lucky he is still living."

My eyebrows rose, and I wondered if the seraph's idea of Nakita teaching me how to use my amulet and me teaching her how to live with her new gift of fear was such a good idea. "Right, but if you want to stay in school, you have to be more subtle."

"Subtle," the reaper mused, her expression easing. "Like a knife up under his ribs?"

Barnabas leaned close. "Change that to a finger, and yes, that would work."

From above me came a tinkling voice at the edge of my

223

awareness. "There once was a girl who had grace."

My attention shot up, and I smiled at the ball of light. "Grace!" I called, hoping no one would think I was talking to the ceiling. The first time a seraph had tried to contact me, I'd passed out from the pain. Now everything came by way of messenger angel, but this was the first time I'd seen Grace.

The angel hovered to land atop the door to my locker. "Hi, Madison. I've got a message for Nakita." Glowing brighter, she added, "What's Barnabas doing here? You're the dark time-keeper, and he's—"

"Not with Ron," Barnabas said, face tight as he crossed his arms over his chest.

The light brightened even more until I had to believe she was visible to everyone. "You went grim!" she exclaimed, and I winced at the pain in my head from the force of her voice.

Barnabas ran a hand over his curls as Nakita sniggered. "I don't know what I am, but I couldn't stay where I was. I don't trust Ron, but I still don't believe in fate."

Nakita flipped her hair back and put a hand on her hip. "You would dare stand in defiance of seraphs?" she almost growled.

He came back with, "I would use my eyes to see and thoughts to think," and Grace hummed impatiently.

Stepping between them, I said, "Okay. Fine! I don't believe in fate, either, but I respect Nakita." *And that big scythe she showed me she could make last week.* "When I'm in school, I'm safe from whatever you guys are worried about.

Why don't you both wait outside?"

Immediately they backed down. "I need to be here," Nakita said, eyes lowered. "For myself. I need to understand. The seraphs are unsure how your being dead will touch upon your ability to read time. And I don't feel right among my own anymore. They think I'm flawed," she finished, and I winced at the shame I could hear in her voice.

Barnabas looked out over the surrounding, excited people, his gaze vacant. "I need something to do. I'm . . . alone too. And you're familiar."

That's nice. I'm familiar. Like an old pair of socks.

"You're both guarding Madison?" Grace asked. "Someone needs to. She wouldn't let me do it."

I felt bad about that, but then she landed on my shoulder and whispered, "Thank you, Madison, for naming me. I thought they were going to take my name from me, but they finally agreed that if I was assigned as a messenger to you permanently, I could keep it."

"Grace, that's great!" I said, truly pleased. It was good to see Grace, but the last time a message had come for Nakita, the dark reaper had excused herself, coming back with a satisfied smile and a new notch on her scythe.

The tiny angel rose high, and I felt a familiar presence behind me. Nakita looked away with her lips pressed together, but Barnabas smiled, and I wasn't surprised when Josh slipped out of the crowd and into our small eddy in the hall traffic.

"Hi, Madison," Josh said as he banged knuckles with Barnabas.

"Hi, Josh." I was nervous, and that made me all the more embarrassed, especially when Grace hummed happily. He looked good, completely recovered from his brush with death. He didn't like Nakita, though, and the feeling was mutual, from what I could tell of her dark expression aimed at the floor.

"Madison is my responsibility," Nakita muttered, continuing our previous conversation. "You failed. Twice. I think you're a spy," she accused Barnabas, ignoring Josh.

The light reaper gone rogue was affronted. "I am not!" he said loudly. "Look at my amulet. Does that look red to you anymore?"

It was true. Much to Barnabas's chagrin, the glow in his amulet had shifted up through the spectrum and was now the bright, neutral gold of an inexperienced reaper. He was no longer tied to Ron. He was tied to me and growing . . . darker.

"If you aren't a spy," Nakita said, her finger pointing, "then why are you here, Barney?"

"Because I don't trust you. And don't call me that."

She hissed something at him, and when Grace went to referee, I turned away, sighing. "They are like little kids," I complained, then smiled. "What lunch do you have?"

"Second," Josh said as he dug out his schedule.

"So do I!" I said, delighted. "I'll meet you at the front water fountain. Unless . . ."

He smiled, making my breath catch. "Unless nothing. I'll be there."

Beside us, Nakita shouted, "I will rip out your tongue and feed it to my hellhounds!"

Josh winced, and a wider space opened between us and everyone else. "Can't you get rid of them?"

Beaming, I shook my head. "Nope. I've tried."

He shifted his book to his other hand. "I think I hear Grace. Is she here? I kind of miss her."

I leaned back against my locker and nodded to Nakita and Barnabas, who were still arguing. People were giving them odd looks, and I wondered if I'd started a new clique. A weird and noisy one. "She brought a message for the almighty 'Kita."

He laughed. It was a nice sound, and I wondered if he would drive me home after school so I wouldn't have to take the bus. That would really melt Amy's retainer.

Josh glanced at Barnabas and Nakita, who had finally stopped arguing so they could listen to Grace. "Are you doing anything after school?"

Not anymore, I thought, but then shrugged. "I don't know. Nakita might have something going on."

"Shut your singing hole," Nakita said to Barnabas, then shook her hair back to find her composure. Facing me, she said, "There's a situation. Barney will watch you for a few . . . hours."

It was as I thought. She had a scything. "Nakita, I don't like this," I said as Barnabas bristled. "Scything people who make bad choices is wrong. It's easy, but wrong."

Her eyebrows arched up. "That's not why they're chosen, and you will feel differently after you have seen enough human atrocity. By the time you learn how to use your amulet, you'll understand. Until then, what you want will make no difference."

That was as about as patronizing as it could get, but she *was* older than everyone here except Barnabas. "What about your domestic studies?" I said, knowing how badly she wanted to fit in, seeing as her own people didn't understand her anymore.

Jaw tight, Nakita handed her class schedule to Josh. "He can do it for me."

Josh's eyebrows went up. "Uh, Nakita. School doesn't work like that."

Barnabas grabbed the paper from Josh and shoved it back at her. "If you go, I go. I'm not going to let you take another soul, so you may as well stay."

"I'd like to see you try to stop me!" she said, starting it all back up again.

Grace dropped between us, a faint shimmer in the air. "All the love in this building! It makes me giddy. I'm out of here. Nakita, are you taking the scythe or not?"

"Yes," she said, and Grace popped out of existence with a burst of inward-falling light and the scent of roses.

Nakita pulled me to her, our heads almost touching. "You should come with me," she said, eyes glancing sideways at the surrounding people. "Perhaps then you will learn how to look forward and see the atrocities this human's choices will bring about. I know you'll agree then."

"It's the first day of school!" I said as Josh started talking to Barnabas to get the scoop on what was going on. "I can't skip the first day of school."

Her blue eyes narrowed and her cheeks flushed. "You are the seraphs' will, Madison."

"Well, the seraphs' will doesn't want to be grounded," I protested, thinking I'd never have believed it possible those words could go together and make sense. "I don't agree with fate," I added. Class was about to start, and the hallway was emptying out.

"It's wrong, Nakita," Barnabas said, loud enough that I worried someone might hear us. "That person has not done anything."

"He will," was her confident answer. "Just because you can't fly high enough to see around corners doesn't mean the seraphs can't."

This was just freaking great. First day of school, and Nakita wanted to take me on a scythe party. The warning bell rang, and I jumped. Sighing, I picked up my books and started down the hall. Josh shifted forward, working his way beside me as Barnabas and Nakita fell in behind.

"So," Josh said, his eyes wide, "are we going to class, or on safari?"

I stared, not believing this. "You want to go too?"

Nakita leaned forward between us, pushing him aside. "You'll enjoy killing this one, Madison. Grace says the demon spawn is going to create a computer virus that takes out the operating systems of a hospital. Hundreds of your precious people, Barnabas, are going to die untimely deaths because of this human's choice made in the search for recognition and pride. If we don't move this soul to a higher plane before he sullies it, he will eventually become a cyberterrorist."

Ooh, strike one.

Barnabas was grim-faced as he came up on my other side. "But he hasn't done it yet. There's always a choice, and he might make the right one."

The hallway was empty. To the right was the hallway that would take me to my physics class, to the left the bright rectangle of the school's front door. "Nakita," I said, my steps slowing in the intersection. "Was I wrong in saving Susan, the girl on the boat?"

"Yes," she said immediately.

"No," Barnabas rejoined.

Nakita held her home ec textbook to her chest, the spreadsheet and bowl of eggs on the cover a weird mix with her severe, almost bloodthirsty expression. "She was going to create articles of truth without compassion. She was going to devote her life to destroying faith and the belief people have in each other. There was no giving in her life, only destruction."

Strike two. "Is that still her fate?" I asked, hearing the *was*.

Her beautiful face shifted, becoming confused. "No," she said, and our steps slowed to a stop. "The seraphs sing that her future is muddied, and they don't know why."

A slow smile curved my lips up. "I do." Pleased, I started for the front doors. I knew now what I was going to do—how I was going to reconcile working as head of a system I didn't agree with until I found my body and returned to normal. "Just like understanding fear changed you, Susan saw death, and as a result, she learned how precious life is. It's hard to make a choice when you can only see one way."

From my left, Barnabas frowned. "You're talking about me," he said sullenly.

"No." I glanced at the front offices, hoping no one was watching. "I don't think so. Maybe?" I shrugged. "I'm going to come with you, Nakita, but before you get your blade out and turn all scary, I want to talk to him."

The dark reaper's eyebrows went high. "Why?" she said, mirroring Barnabas's confused expression.

"To see if I can't change his fate," I said. *Duh . . .*

Okay, so I was dead, my body was somewhere between now and the next, and I had two argumentative reapers guarding me from the very timekeeper I'd once trusted. Things weren't all bad. My dad didn't have a clue I was dead, Josh was alive, and until I got my body back and got off this roller coaster, I not only could skip school with impunity, but it was my moral responsibility to do so.

We had reached the door, and I yanked it open. Sunlight spilled in, warming me as Josh caught the door and held it. "You're going to skip?" he asked, and I grinned.

"Yup. Nakita and Barnabas can cover for me. For us. For a good girl, I certainly do some bad things."

Josh laughed as he gestured for me to go first. "Breaking rules isn't bad when what you're doing is more important than the rule itself."

I hesitated on the threshold, squinting in the sun. "You think it makes a difference?"

Josh nodded, and his smile made a quiver start in the pit of my being. "Yeah. I do."

"Me too," I said, and together, we walked out into the sun to save some good guy's soul.

EXTRAS

Once Dead, Twice Shy
A NOVEL

Are you a light or dark reaper?
Take the Fate or Free Will quiz!

Madison's glossary to the world of angels and reapers

What's on Madison's iPod?

A sneak peek at how Madison's destiny
(or something like it) unfolds in Kim Harrison's
next book, *Early to Death, Early to Rise*

Fate or chance? Free will or destiny? Are you a light or dark reaper?

Madison never believed in that stuff—that is, until a dark reaper targeted her for an early death because of something he saw in her future. And she's still not convinced! Not sure what you believe? Take the quiz below to find out.

1. The car directly in front of you gets into a fender bender. You breathe a sigh of relief and think what?
   a. Good thing I'm such a good driver or it could have been me!
   b. A guardian angel must have been watching over me.

2. Your favorite store is having an amazing sale and you expect everything to be picked over. You arrive and the only things left are all in your size! What thought passes through your mind?
   a. I'm glad I got here before this awesome dress got snatched up!
   b. This dress was totally made for me—the stars really aligned in my favor today!

3. At your favorite coffee shop you order your usual and take a seat. The barista brings you the wrong order and you discover that your delicious coffee was given to the equally delicious guy by the window. Your first reaction is:
   a. The barista is having an off day, but now you have

a reason to strike up a conversation.

b. I might have the wrong coffee, but fate handed me a super-cute guy.

4. You are five minutes late for curfew and you know your parents will flip. As you open the door ready to explain, you see them both asleep in their recliners with a movie on. You just avoided a long lecture and think which of the following?

a. No wonder they're asleep. . . . Those black-and-white movies are always a snooze-fest.

b. Lucky Charms is definitely the breakfast of this champion!

5. Math is your nemesis and you totally didn't study enough for the test next period. When you walk into class you see a substitute teacher and a note saying the test has been canceled because your teacher is out sick. After you leap for joy you turn to your friend and say:

a. "Hope this flu bug visits our gym teacher, too. I really want out of kickball!"

b. "Um, am I standing in a beam of light right now?"

If you got mostly As:
In the balancing act between light and dark, you lean toward the light.

You are not wasting your change by throwing it into some wishing well. For you, there's no hidden meaning behind why things happen. People make choices and no amount of rabbit feet will change the outcome. You believe the old saying, "The only sure thing about luck is that it will change."

If you got mostly Bs:

In the balancing act between light and dark, you lean toward the dark.

Fate, destiny, or fortune—call it whatever you want, but you believe things happen for a reason. Each person has a destiny to fulfill; of course you hope your destiny includes a super-cute guy! Every fortune cookie you crack open may give you a clue as to what lies ahead.

Once Dead, Twice Shy Glossary of Terms

Now that she's dead, Madison has even more vocab to learn than she did in high school English. What's a black wing? What do amulets do, exactly? Here's what's on her flash cards in the afterlife.

Dark reapers: Reapers who Kairos sends to kill people when the probable future shows that they are going to make decisions contrary to the grand schemes of fate.

Light reapers: Reapers who Ron sends to save those people from an untimely death, to ensure humanity's right of free will.

Timekeepers: Both the light and dark reapers have their own timekeeper. Each one is responsible for watching the strands of time to determine when a person must be scythed—or saved.

Amulet: A stonelike necklace that makes it possible to communicate beyond the earth's sphere. Each amulet has its own aura or song that matches with its owner.

Black wings: Creatures that feed on the souls of those killed by dark reapers, typically appearing right before a scything takes place. Most of the time they go unnoticed by the living, but they can resemble crows when a soul is in danger.

A *Killer* Soundtrack

A girl's gotta have a great soundtrack if she's going to walk the line between the living and the dead, all the while battling reapers, avoiding black wings, and oh yeah, finding time to flirt with her cute crush. What's on Madison's iPod as she attempts to take control of her destiny once and for all? Take a peek at her fave kick-butt playlist!

No Doubt—"Just a Girl"

30 Seconds to Mars—"Kings and Queens"

Ozzy Osbourne—"Not Going Away"

Toyko Police Club—"Your English Is Good"

Dashboard Confessional—"Hands Down"

Nirvana—"Lake of Fire"

The Kooks—"Always Where I Need to Be"

The Bravery—"Believe"

New Order—"True Faith"

Vampire Weekend—"The Kids Don't Stand a Chance"

Foo Fighters—"Times Like These"

White Rabbits—"Percussion Gun"

Green Day—"Holiday"

Nickelback—"Photograph"

**A sneak peek at how Madison's destiny
(or something like it) unfolds in Kim Harrison's
next book, *Early to Death, Early to Rise***

Prologue

Seventeen, dead, and in charge of heaven's dark angels—all itching to kill someone. Yup, that's me, Madison, the new dark timekeeper without a clue. It wasn't exactly how I envisioned my "higher education" going the night I blew off my junior prom and died at the bottom of a ravine. I'd survived my death by stealing my murderer's amulet.

Now it's my responsibility to send a dark reaper to end a person's earthly existence. The idea is to save their soul at the cost of their life. Fate, the seraphs would say. But I don't believe in fate; I believe in choice, which means I'm in charge of the very people I once fought against.

The seraphs are confused about the changes I'm trying to make to a system I don't believe in, but they're willing to give me a chance. At least, that's the theory. The reality is a bit more . . . complicated.

One

The car was hot from the sun, and I pulled my fingertips from it as I slunk past. Excitement layered itself over my skin like a second aura. Hunched and furtive, I followed Josh in his first-day-of-school jeans and tucked-in shirt as he wove through the parking lot toward his truck. Yes, it was the first day of school, and yes, we were ditching, but it wasn't like anyone ever *did* anything the first day. Besides, I thought the seraphs would forgive me; it was one of their marked souls I was going to try to save.

Josh turned to me as he stopped, crouched behind a red Mustang as he tossed his blond hair from his eyes and grinned. It was obvious this wasn't his first time skipping. It wasn't the only time I'd ditched school, either, but I'd never done it with a posse. I smiled back, but as Josh's gaze went behind me, his smile faded.

"She's going to get us caught," he muttered.

My yellow sneakers with the skull-and-crossbones shoelaces ground into the pavement as I turned to look. Barnabas was skulking properly between the cars, his dark eyes serious and his expression grim. Nakita, though, was casually strolling, her arms swinging and her perfection absolute. She was wearing a pair of my designer jeans and one of my short tops, looking better than I ever could, with her dark hair shining and her black toenails glinting in the glorious sun. She hadn't painted them that color, it was natural. Normally I'd hate Nakita for her looks alone, but the dark reaper didn't have a clue how pretty she was.

Halting in a crouch beside me, Barnabas frowned, the scent of feathers and sunflowers coming off him. The angel masquerading as a high school senior in his faded black jeans and even more faded band T-shirt was twice fallen: first when he was kicked out of heaven untold millennia ago, and now for having switched sides in the middle of heaven's war.

"Nakita hasn't the faintest idea how to do this," the reaper grumbled, brushing his frizzy brown curls out of his eyes and squinting. The two had been on opposite ends of heaven's war, and it didn't take much to set them off on each other now.

I cringed, waving for Nakita to crouch down, but she just kept walking. Nakita was my official guardian, assigned to me by the seraphs.

Technically, as the dark timekeeper, I was her boss. Although in all things earthly I was the smart one, she knew my job and what I was supposed to be doing. Trouble was, I didn't want to do it heaven's way. I had other ideas.

"Get down, you ninny!" Barnabas hissed, and the petite, beautiful, and deadly girl looked behind her, confused. Over her shoulder was the trendy purse I'd given her this morning to complete her look. It matched her red sandals and was absolutely empty, but she insisted on carrying it because she thought it helped her blend in.

"Why?" she said as she approached. "If someone should stop us, I'll simply smite them."

Smite? I thought, wincing. She hadn't been on earth very long. Barnabas fit in better, having been kicked out of heaven before the pyramids were built because he believed in choice, not fate, but Nakita once told me rumor had it he'd been ousted for falling in love with a human girl.

"Nakita," I said, pulling at her when she got close, and she obediently dropped to a crouch, her long hair swinging. "No one uses that word anymore."

"It's a perfectly fine word," she said, affronted.

"Maybe you could try smacking people instead?" Josh suggested.

Barnabas frowned. "Don't encourage her," he muttered.

Nakita stood. "We should go," she said, looking about. "If you can't get the mark to *choose* a better path before Ron sends a light reaper to keep him alive, I'm going to take his soul to save it."

With that, Nakita started walking for Josh's truck. "Take his soul" was a nice way of saying "kill him." The enormity of what I was trying to do fell on me, and my shoulders slumped.

I was the new dark timekeeper, but unlike the dark keepers who came before me, I didn't believe in fate. I believed in choice. The entire situation was a big cosmic joke—apart from the bit about me being dead. The old dark timekeeper thought that killing me, his foretold replacement, would give him immortality. No one had known who I was until it was too late to change anything, and I'd been stuck with the job until I could find my real body and break the bond with the amulet that kept me alive without it.

Josh rose, peering at the parking lot's entrance through the Mustang's windows. "Come on. Let's get to my truck before she takes the front seat. I'm not driving with her riding shotgun."

Knees bent and keeping in a crouch, we started after her. Barnabas was vastly better at this soul-saving stuff than I was, knowing how to use his amulet and having experience finding people marked for an early death in order to save them from reapers like Nakita. That he had switched sides to stay with me was as weird as my being chosen as the new dark timekeeper to begin with. Maybe it was guilt that had kept him with me, since he'd failed to keep me alive when I'd been targeted for death. Perhaps it was anger at his old boss, Ron, the light timekeeper, who'd lied to both of us in his quest for supremacy. Or it might possibly be that Barnabas thought I had answers for the questions that Ron's betrayal had raised. Whatever the reason, I was glad Barnabas was here. Neither of us agreed with heaven's philosophy of killing someone before they went bad, but if I'd been fated to become the new dark timekeeper, I could've done far worse than win Barnabas's loyalty. Nakita didn't trust him and thought he was a spy.

"Uh, guys?" Josh said, and I froze when I followed his gaze to the squad car parked before the school. Beside it was a woman in uniform, hands on her hips and looking our way.

"Crap!" I yelped, dropping. Josh was right beside me, and Barnabas had never risen above the level of the car. "Get down!" I almost hissed at Nakita, and yanked her toward the pavement. My pulse hammered. Okay, I know. I was dead, but try telling my mind that. It thought I was alive, and with the tactile illusion of a body, who was I to tell it different? It was embarrassing. If I was simply sitting, nothing—but the minute I got excited, the memory of my pulse started up. It was so unfair that I had to deal with all the physical crap of being scared when I was already dead.

New York Times bestselling author **KIM HARRISON** was born and raised in the upper Midwest but has since fled south to better avoid snow. She spends her time tending orchids, cooking with some guy in a leather jacket, and training her dog. Her current vices include good chocolate and exquisite sushi. Kim is the author of the bestselling Hollows series, and she contributed to the paranormal collection PROM NIGHTS FROM HELL. You can visit her online at www.kimharrison.net.